The Wood of Suicides

LAURA ELIZABETH WOOLLETT

The
Wood
of
Suicides

THE PERMANENT PRESS
Sag Harbor, NY 11963

For information, address:
  The Permanent Press
  4170 Noyac Road
  Sag Harbor, NY 11963
  www.thepermanentpress.com

Library of Congress Cataloging-in-Publication Data

  Woollett, Laura Elizabeth—
    The Wood of Suicides / Laura Elizabeth Woollett.
      pages cm
    ISBN 978-1-57962-350-0
      1. Teenage girls—Fiction. 2. Boarding schools—Fiction.
    3. Self-realization in women—Fiction. 4. Psychological fiction.
    5. Love stories. I. Title.

  PS3623.O7127W66 2014
  813'.6—dc23   2013039996

Printed in the United States of America

ACKNOWLEDGEMENTS

This book could not have existed without the love, patience, indulgence, and hilarious annotations of Kirill Kovalenko; the excellent advice and unfailing kindness of my agent Victoria Marini; the vision of Marty and Judith Shepard; and the nurture, support, and diversion provided by my family and friends in Perth and Melbourne. I would like to thank you all for helping me to bring my first novel into the world.

When the fierce soul makes its way from a body,
From which it has managed to rip itself out . . .
It falls into the wood, there is no choice of place;

—DANTE ALIGHIERI, *The Divine Comedy*

She had hardly ended her prayer when a heavy numbness
came over her body; her soft white bosom was ringed
in a layer of bark, her hair was turned into foliage,
her arms into branches.

—OVID, *Metamorphoses*

PROLOGUE

What did Daphne see, when her arms hardened into boughs and her world was choked with green?

Was there a nymph's wading pool, heavily chlorinated? Was there an overhang of pink and purple wisteria? Was there summer hysteria? Was there a hovel of hornets, ready to attack at the slightest whiff of pheromone or even a woman's perfume? Was there the distant thump of a car door? A Pacific breeze? Was there a weeping willow? A god reciting poetry?

Girls turning into trees. Trees pecked at by harpies. This is all I see.

PART ONE

My name is Laurel Marks and I am the daughter of one of those impossible unions: the intellectual man and the sensuous woman. I suppose this means that I'm blessed from a genetic standpoint, getting the best of both mind and physicality. For all this, I can't help seeing myself as an evolutionary dead-end.

I grew up in Lower Pacific Heights, in a Victorian townhouse—less grand, though as tasteful as any of the mansions of Pacific Heights proper. For me, it provided an almost immaterial world of dust motes and slanted sunlight and telebabble in the next room. My mother pottered about in the background with part-time work and yearly renovations. She wore a lot of white in those days, white dresses that billowed like drapes. She painted cherry blossoms, drove me to dance and deportment classes that I failed to complete. I was, quite idyllically, an only child.

I liked to believe that I was raised in the style of the Germans. A psychologist (Ainsworth) once remarked on the huge number of anxious-avoidant attachments found among German infants. Defensive posture. Limited emotional expression. A preference for solitary play. Avoidant adults would rather be independent than intimate with another person.

My father's parents came from Trier, in the Rhineland-Palatinate. My grandfather's surname was "Marx," though he was neither a Jew nor a socialist. My grandmother was born

"Dreyfuss"—literally "from Trier." My mother's side of the family were ruddy, pleasant Irish people with some money and no other children besides her. I always gave more authority to my German heritage, probably because it seemed somehow essential to my character: my obedience, my perverseness, my craving for order and patriarchy.

I attended a nearby Catholic girls' school every year with the exception of my last, when circumstances led me to become a boarder. My grades were good, As and Bs for the most part, though admittedly not what they could have been. I was quiet and disliked everybody, yet managed to fit in—if only because I was too indolent to do otherwise. Report cards praised my mature and consistent approach.

He was a non-interventionist god. A god who was impotent. A god who may or may not have seen everything but, in any case, never appeared to be looking when I sought out his sloe-dark eyes. A god whose image I was made in, perhaps, but imperfectly, impulsively, in a sticky, blind moment of self-purgation. A god whose presence was stronger in his absence. Could I call him a god?

In the mornings, my father and I would both sit at the same table, drinking our coffee black and with two sachets of sweetener. A rare, intimate day would have me asking him a question: "What is Occam's razor?" or "Do you think Dostoyevsky was an existentialist?" I would watch the angular patterns that he made with his hands, delighting secretly in our infrequent eye contact and his deliberate, droning speech.

My father's working hours were unpredictable and extensive. Nevertheless, there were times when I came home early in the afternoon to find him reading on the daybed: fully clad in two-piece suit and tasseled loafers and totally indifferent to my truancy, as if I were just another of his faceless coeds.

The college where he taught was, like my own school, only a matter of blocks away from the family home. I was in the habit of skipping many classes in the afternoons, too dazed by the schoolyard dust, surrounding chatter, and my own self-enforced starvation to endure the stretch of the day. Often, I didn't go to school at all, but simply stayed in bed until both parents had left the house for work. My hours alone passed without the slightest thought or action, workbooks open all around me unread, as I lay prone in the indoor sun.

It was not uncommon for me to take my homework to the room with the daybed, knowing that it was his favorite and that he was in the habit of stopping there to put his brief-case down when he came home from work. I took pleasure in looking more studious than I was and would ignore him as he came in, my head down over the open pages. I often kept my uniform on well into the evening in order to better look the part for him. White button-up blouse. Maroon sweater. Gray skirt. Black hosiery. By the time I began reading *Hamlet* for eleventh grade English literature, I was filling out my uniform nicely, and he developing another habit, of glancing over my shoulder whenever he passed by to see what I was studying.

The west-facing windows meant that it was a room for indoor plants and flower arrangements, as well as shelf upon shelf of legal dictionaries and publications. Medical books also began to show up in that room, in later years, with emphasis on the subjects of nervous-system pathology, neurosurgery, neuro-pharmacology, and cranial nerve disease. Detailed anatomical drawings showed faces split open, to reveal brainstems, ganglia, nerve divisions, and the sore teeth to which all this was connected.

I WONDER now if he'd been a virgin when he met my mother. Though I realize this isn't the sort of thing a daughter should be asking, in light of his actions, it would explain a lot. The briefness of their courtship. The perfunctory outdoor ceremony. The blatant sensuality of his choice in partner. My main difficulty is in trying to conceive of their initial connection. A frolicsome *artiste*-to-turn-interior-decorator and reticent young professor, united by mutual acquaintances at some crowded summer soiree.

By the time I came along, they were obviously familiar enough. She would ask him whether he knew that Margaret Pratchett was having her kitchen decorated, whether he thought it odd that she was not asked to help with the décor. She would joggle her dainty, high-arched feet (whose pronation I inherited, though I lost out on the daintiness) and moan about the weather or the construction workers outside. The man abided it all without complaint, eyeing her feet and flipping the pages of his students' papers.

Like my mother, he'd been brought up by elderly kin. Unlike her, a pandered only child and minor miracle (parents in their forties, presumed infertile), his growing conditions had been severe. Grandparents from the old country. A brittle, nervous mother who died during childbirth and a blue-collar father who took to drinking soon after. He had compensated as high-achievers do—debating team, essay competitions, scholarship to Stanford—and was already starting his clerkship by the time my grandfather succumbed to cirrhosis.

He had a handsome if unmemorable sort of face—sharp-jawed, straight-nosed, dark-eyed and browed—with an impressively high forehead. His hands, like my own, were long and exquisite, though masculinized by roped veins that carried up his arms and, I assume, back toward his unknowable heart. His lineaments were trim, functional, touching in their very austerity. He held himself tall and erect and, despite his ectomorphy, exhibited a perfect, V-shaped torso. His body hair was sparse and his skin a couple of von Luschan tones darker than my own.

He spoke in a low-pitched monotone, simultaneously stirring and difficult to make out. In his last decade, he often had problems with tooth pain, which proved later on to be of an entirely different nature. After the extraction of all the molars on his left side and the continuing trigeminal pain, he chewed with only one side of his mouth. I liked to think that I understood, through some secret attunement to suffering, the dark crescents of his under-eyes, the convict stubble of his jaw—prior to the pain, he had always been clean-shaven—and the spasms that occasionally caused his calm face to contort.

She didn't suffer, so couldn't have understood. She handed him glasses of water to wash down the pills, and his packet of Dunhills (the smoking was a recent thing, to speed up the action of his anticonvulsants; meanwhile, he'd given up alcohol altogether). Her hands were as soft and dainty as her feet. She was like a modern-day Mary Magdalene, or perhaps a Botticellian Venus: sea-green eyes, cupid-bow lips, scarlet curls of a meretrix. She also had a pair of dimples on her lower back, I knew, from the countless times I sat in on her dressing as a child. I was fascinated, once upon a time, by the lingerie drawer, and by the eau de parfum, which she spritzed all over her breasts and torso (not only the traditional pulse points at the wrists and throat). Married at twenty-three, widowed at forty-one, she maintained herself wonderfully over those eighteen years of wifehood.

In my own mind, it may not have been true love, but it was a nice arrangement. He gave her a large cut of his paycheck, enough to keep her occupied while he was writing his law reviews or rereading *The Nicomachean Ethics*. On weekend mornings, her moaning could be heard—high, delicate, persistent—from behind their bedroom door. The arrangement was liberal, almost aristocratic: the old world academic in his ivory tower, with the fresh, frivolous wife at his beck and call.

I wanted to believe that it was nothing more than an arrangement, that a god so cold, so rational, would never fall prey to anything as base as passion. Let us say they loved well: the ring fit and they procreated. I was born in the summertime, August 1985—the product of the god and the woman.

OF COURSE, my virginity is far more relevant than my father's.

I was a Pre-Raphaelite's dream come true. Auburn hair, partway down my back, undulating and prone to flyaways. Deep-set almond eyes, which could morph from a rich, almost oriental black to a light-sodden leprosy of green and brown when I cried. My cheekbones were shaded, my brows dark, my pout petal-pink and obstinately wistful. I had the curious nose of any decent nymph, the pallid face, and the unwieldy, intellectual hands.

I was devoid of muscle tone and with my adamant, teen-aged tendency not to eat much, invariably got dizzy toward the end of the day. At seventeen, my BMI was exactly level with my age; nevertheless, softnesses persisted. My backside had a stubborn layer of female fat, which no amount of skipped lunches could do away with. Although the prongs of my hips were sharp enough to bruise a man during sex, they were also shaped for childbearing. I had regular periods from the age of twelve and a half onward. My breasts were small and pretty, with areole the same color as my mouth.

I resented my body, even as I was entranced by it. I knew that its lushness was merely a semblance, disguising deep putre-faction, death. My warm breath was a funeral dirge. My bur-nished waves were the dead leaves of autumn. My smell was oversweet, with a catch of something acrid. As with all things green, my charm wasn't in my freshness itself, but the certainty that it couldn't last.

FOR SEVENTEEN years, I shuffled through life: a life that was little more than a small eternity of lunchless lunch hours, hunger headaches, and a school within walking distance of my empty house. Weekdays held about as much interest and variation for me as the single slice of dry toast I started them with. My teachers rarely remarked upon my absences; my peers, still less. There is a sense of deliverance that I still associate with exiting past back buildings and strolling downhill, through dappled sun and shade, past the mansions and glass-fronted boutiques of Fillmore Street. On days like this, I could slip through the front door with a silvery clatter of keys and walk straight into the sunlit room where my father was aching.

The sunlit room with its lily vases, ashtrays, hanging spider plants, and smell of dust and sweat. Silverfish crawling out of the oldest books.

It happened now and then that I would come home while he was off work, nursing one of his "toothaches," and would be obliged to fetch him his pain pills. The light would be coming in; impurities would be spotlighted inside the flower vases. His eyes would be screwed shut, either for the intensity of the sunlight or the intensity of his pain. I was aware that he barely distinguished between my mother and me in that state, in the midst of those throes that almost resembled ecstasy.

I would bring him his pill with water, never daring enough to bring his Dunhills as well. He would hold me there occasionally until the spasm was over, forcefully grasping at my arm or hand. The first time this happened, I almost jumped out of my skin—I was so unused to him touching me without warning. I was prepared, however, for following occasions: even found myself easing enough to reciprocate the contact. If he clenched my hand, I would clench his in return. If he clasped my arm, I would clasp one of his arms too. From above, I would observe the silvery sheen of his gritted teeth, the details of his grooming and how he had let it slip. When it was over, I would extricate myself gently, always careful not to rouse him by rising from the daybed too soon.

My movements conspired with his illness to blur the boundaries between wife and daughter. I had always believed that if he were to love me, really love me, it would be for the properties I shared with him, not because of any resemblance to her. It was becoming clearer to me, however, that one could not afford to be scrupulous in matters of love. I began to fantasize about using my likeness to her as a means of winning him over: of pulling down the blinds in the sunroom, watching him wash down his pills, and wafting over him like a sensuous phantom, like the smoke from the cigarettes I would bring to him immediately after.

I WAS two months away from my seventeenth birthday when he turned forty-four. The event fell on a Saturday, which meant that she did not lead him out of the bedroom until close to midday, looking charmingly shabby with his dark beard and ill-buttoned white shirt. I slit my eyes at her as she sat him down at the kitchen table, with a coquettish kiss on the forehead and ruffle of his bed hair. "Stay right there, birthday boy." She squeezed his shoulders, before turning around and busying herself with his breakfast.

Unlike them, I was already bathed and dressed. I had wrapped up a copy of *Civilization and Its Discontents* in the original German, purchased weeks ago from the foreign-language bookstore. Though it was not my favorite of Freud's works, I thought he'd appreciate the fact that it had won a Goethe prize. Picking up the package, I tiptoed over to where he sat and bent down to brush my lips lightly over his bristled cheek. It was the first time in months that I had kissed him and I was careful to do so as softly as possible. At the moment of contact, however, my father flinched and cursed as that whole side of his face was crippled by a lightning bolt of pain. "For Christ's sake, Laurel!"

My mother set down the French press with a clatter and rushed to his side. "Oh, Jonathon! Jonathon, darling, I'm here," she cooed into his ear, groping for his veiny left hand. Her softer, paler hand nestled inside his. In the midday light, his wedding band sparkled triumphantly. A gold crucifix glistened between her unfettered breasts.

I stood aside, casting my eyes down at the unopened Freud. It was obvious to me that she was to blame for the attack. She had clearly overtaxed his nerves with the excesses of that morning.

I HAD loved my mother once, passionately and indecently: loved with the love of a creature that is all body, and that depends on the body of another to survive. I had loved her, but early on I outgrew her, and my love soured like milk into something that resembled contempt.

He had never known his mother. Whatever he may have needed from her was supplied by bottled formula and Oma Marx, with her thick calves and coiled gray bun. That he was never truly nurtured may explain his asceticism as an adult; then again, it may also explain his attraction to my mother, and that milky-white hourglass figure of hers, with its balanced C-cups—the very embodiment of nourishment.

He proposed to her only five months after they met at a friend's summer party. She had gone there barefoot, wearing only a white caftan, as if she could not afford to dress herself—although her pedicure told him otherwise. The pair were wedded in the April of 1984, in the Japanese gardens, when the cherry trees were in bloom. They honeymooned in Kyoto, feeding on seaweed, horseradish, and salmon roe, and sleeping late on a low futon bed behind the shoji. Their love was self-contained, absolute; it demanded no interference. I was conceived all the same. For that, I could never forgive them.

Snapshots from before I was born show my parents as I always knew them: degagé, in love. I was not a planned baby, but a happy accident, which prompted her well-off parents to make a deposit on what was to become the family home as a blessing. The photographs taken during her pregnancy all reveal the couple's exhilaration, their high hopes, and my mother looking like a figure from Botticelli's *Primavera*. In pictures from my infancy, however, they're just an inexpert pair in their twenties, dazed and stiffly clutching their dribble-chinned baby girl.

My first distinct memories come from when I was a toddler, aged two or three. The earliest: a dinner party at the home of another young married couple, where the adults drank together and I was thrust among my peers until—teetering into the winey, hazy, high-ceilinged room—my mother took me precariously onto her knee. Another, also a party: at a foreign patio, with crêpe paper, dream catcher, marijuana fumes, and women congregated incongruously around a chocolate fountain. My father appears rarely, if ever, in these early remembrances of mine: little more than a moving shadow; a dull, indecipherable baritone; a hand cinching the fabric of her waist.

The nineties: their decade in Arcadia. Weekends they would doze in a heap while I watched cartoons in the den, eating dry cereal with the blinds unpulled. Our house was rife with art, with freshly bought flowers, which mingled in a fatal way with the relics of his intellect. I watched petals fall over musty tomes, saw his eyeglasses abandoned atop her feminine, Art Nouveau furniture (spindle-legs, stained-glass panels, and everywhere, transparent dragonflies). Or else I would get a glimpse of her flitting into the kitchen in only her silk oriental dressing gown—a glimpse I would pretend not to see, staring fixedly at the screen.

As a free-spirited woman in her thirties, she was far more comfortable in her skin than I would have liked. When we were home alone, it was a habit for her to leave the bathroom door partly open during her shower and post-shower sprucing. To stop the mirror misting up or simply to allow her little girl to talk to her freely—it was a motherly nudity, spontaneous and confidential. In the yellowish lighting, her slick skin had the look of candle wax; her private flame would peek through the arc of a raised leg, to which she strenuously applied moisturizing lotion. Breasts bobbed innocuously. I knew that if my father were home she would have had the courtesy to close the door, to have at least a semblance of shame.

Although as a very young girl, I may have been enthralled by such displays of beautification, by the time that I reached a certain age, I began to find it abnormal, to take offense to the assumed intimacies between mother and daughter. A catty remark, of the sort only a seemingly innocent eight-year-old can make ("*Can't* you close the door, Mom?") soon set her straight, however, creating a new and welcome barrier between us. I had acquired my sense of asceticism over the years, as my consciousness broadened, becoming increasingly disconcerted by matters of the flesh.

My asceticism was different from his, in that it was a rebellion against excess and not, as I suspect was the case with him, a defense against deprivation. I was clean. I craved order. I shrank from the sluttish untidiness of her red hair clogging up the drains. Because he had been deprived, I knew that I should not condemn him too harshly for that hypocrisy—a hypocrisy brought on by love, or the Darwinian need to procreate.

I myself resolved never to be a hypocrite, to need no one, to remain forever a being of pure mind. But alas, what hope did I really have, when I was only half the god, half the mind that he was? When the other half of me was *she*?

The fallacy of conception: two halves join and expect to make a whole.

A turning point came the year that I turned ten, 1995, when he presented at a conference in Cambridge—afterward taking her on a tour of Western and Central Europe without me. I passed the month with my maternal grandmother in Fremont who, at almost eighty, was forced to withstand the worst of my ingratitude. Moping on the carpet, tracing meticulous maps of the continent, I spent my days imagining obsolete Moravia, glittering Bohemia, thatched rooftops and railroads passing over the black heart of Germany: ancient things, beautiful things, that were absolutely forbidden to me.

They were back in four weeks, burdened with art books, tissue-wrapped figurines, and a honeymoon glow that I resented (they had no right to be happy, I told myself, when everybody knew that they'd been doing dirty things in their hotel rooms). A poster of Klimt's *The Kiss* was framed for our collection—how closely that blissful redhead resembled her!—while, unbeknownst to them, I destroyed the gorgeous, genuine Italian charm bracelet they had chosen as a gift for me.

I found bad omens in their photographs, though they looked innocent enough. Them pausing on bridges. Them in casual dress. Them blinking at churches and obelisks. In my eyes, their innocence was a testament to their guilt—for only the guilty could be so ignorant, so happy, for all my brute knowledge and unhappiness. The cold fury with which I regarded their artifacts and answered her maddening queries ("Did you have fun at Grandma's?" "Did you go to the water park?" "Were you well-behaved?") did not abate with time, but merely descended deep within me, adding to my ever-growing animosity.

The following year, my mother's mother died: ostensibly from stomach cancer, truthfully from the callous conduct of her one and only grandchild. On the day of the service, I couldn't stand the sight of myself in the mirror, eleven years old and intolerably ugly, with my snub nose and ill-fitting dress. I kicked up a storm about having to attend, which is one of the few times that I recall being disciplined. Afterward, I watched as my mother strode to the door, stiff with emotion—her hand burning with the heat of my impertinence, her eyes burning with tears (both of our eyes, actually, but only hers too disgusted to seek mine). I rubbed my face and looked over at him, hoping for a glimpse of acknowledgement, something conspiring in his eye to tell me that she had acted wrongly. My father was impassive, however. In the hallway, with his hands in his pockets, he returned my gaze without any expression whatsoever, the hypocrite. They turned to wait outside together for the funeral car, and neither paid any heed as I obediently picked up my purse and wiped at my eyes.

How COULD they be so cruel, so supercilious? How could they, when I knew better than they who they were, what they did, what they were composed of? I had pried in their cupboards. I had found their pile of books. The Art of Sexual Ecstasy. Taoist Secrets of Love. Tantra in Practice. Not to mention the purely pictorial guides. Contortionists. Perverts. Westerners with Eastern predilections. Never mind that they sent me to a school of the Sacred Heart, that we went as a family to mass on Easter and Christmas Eve. All of that was just appearances. I had always believed in God, an intellectual and appetite-less God who would not allow me to be sullied. How could he be trusted to keep me clean, however, when he could not even keep himself from being defiled? Because I was a masochist, because I was compelled to know my enemies, to immerse myself completely in the things I hated most, I read those books. All of them. As thoroughly as I could with the mind of a twelve-year-old. Those books, I believe, more than anything else, were to blame for my unerring preference for doing things "the Christian way" in my first months of love. For all my sins, I tried to be a good Christian.

PROFESSOR JONATHON MARKS: June 22, 1958—August 16, 2002:

Jonathon Ulrich Marks was born in Anaheim on June 22, 1958, the son of Emmanuel and Marie Marks (née Dreyfuss). A precocious student, he earned a Juris Doctor from Stanford University in 1978. After graduation, Jonathon spent several years clerking for Judge Alfred Browning of the Ninth Circuit Court of Appeals in San Francisco. In 1983, Jonathon began his career with UC Hastings, rising to the rank of full professor in 1990. He was the author of three books, A Condensed

History of Legal Philosophy *(1992)*, Modern Jurisprudence and its Aristotelian Foundations *(1997)*, *and* New Traditions in Natural Law *(2001)*. *Jonathon's life ended tragically on August 16, 2002, after a three-year battle with trigeminal neuralgia. He is survived by his loving wife Elizabeth and their daughter Laurel.*

I was her daughter, yes, but how passionately I denied it! Even my beauty attempted to suppress hers, making me mousy for more years than I could ever be considered attractive. I was comfortable in my plainness, as children of an ascetic persuasion tend to be: taking my Eucharist, studying the female saints, praying, in the belief that the inconsistencies I suffered through would someday be corrected. All my instincts were driven together, into a single urge for consistency, which hoped to see me emerge—shining, superior—over the Eternal Damnation of the hypocrites. I was pure, I was meek, I did not take lightly the claim that I would one day inherit the earth. I believed, and so my resentment became creed.

He had not felt the hypocrisy of being the man that he was and being with a woman like her. His punishment was felt, however—a jolt from within, a splitting of earth, by way of the trigeminal nerve; a punishment that *I* had willed. And yet, it was impossible for me to rejoice in my strength; in my new, shining body with its perceptibly reddening hair. Everything about this body weighed down on me, as heavy and dark as lead—hinting at my own doom, my own inevitable hypocrisy.

In vain, I tried to educate myself, to take arms against fate. Self-knowledge was my defense. It comforted me to know that my personality was anal-retentive; that an oral fixation led me to be irrationally independent, self-denying, and prey to eating disorders; that issues in my phallic stage meant that I was sexually repressed. Then there was the undeniable fact of my Electra complex.

There was a time when I had only been aware of them, the entity. What I discovered about myself, however, forced me to view him in a new light. Suddenly, my father stood out to me as an object worthy of fixation. He was a safe love object, someone I could love without contradiction. Moreover, I reasoned, my love would do him good as well. Through my chastity, he would at last be cleansed, cured of the ailments her sensuality had induced.

I began to make my advances, to develop my arts, to place myself in his path. Every day, I became more refined, more enticing, more incomprehensible—in short, more of a woman. At home, I went about in my stocking feet, drawing in my toes to accentuate my arches. I adopted ways of sitting with my legs stretched out before me and my spine against the daybed, or lying and reading on my stomach with my back and feet arched, emphasizing curves. There were times when I felt sure that he was looking; sure that he saw it all, and was not exactly sickened. In the end, however, my father was a sick man; too sick to survive the sheer, dark force of my fixation.

THE MEDICINE cabinet. Labels to read. Side-effects, including: dizziness, drowsiness, dryness of the mouth, nausea, diarrhea, constipation, headaches, aching joints, muscular pain, loss of appetite, and impotence. The opiates were all gone, on his person at the time, presumably confiscated. All that remained were the anticonvulsants, antidepressants, and muscle relaxants, along with his abandoned shaving kit, his neglected toothbrush, and the cologne and alcohol-free mouthwash upon which he had become dependent.

Having found what I wanted, I closed the cabinet door, avoiding my reflection. I made my way back through their room, trying not to be arrested by the marital bed, with all its associations, or by that particular Caravaggio print in the hall (*Judith Beheading Holofernes*), which made me sick with guilt. I recalled how she would pass that painting on weekend mornings in her dressing gown, with a laden breakfast tray—coffee, cream, Splenda, piled toast with marmalade, and a single plucked marigold, her feminine touch—shutting the door before I could see him sitting up, all scant chest hair and sheet-draped loins.

Their bed was a wrought-iron queen canopy, with wadded, white bedcovers and a thin, white awning. How frequently those sheets were rumpled, that air darkened with the aromas of their sex . . . and yet, it was a holy room, a matrimonial room, a room from which I understood my exclusion. Potpourri in tiny china bowls along the dresser-bureau, and perfumes in tiny glass bottles. The glass of the vanity, and her reflection in it as she recapped her perfume or selected some bit of jewelry— a brooch, a ring, a bracelet, from the Japanese hand-painted chest with the many drawers, or a necklace, stolen from the body of Christ himself. For there was a sizeable antique crucifix that stood by the mirror, draped in the fine chains that had strayed from her jewelry chest. A Christ draped in gold and silver, looking almost as thin as my father had been.

The smaller crucifix that oversaw his coffin was not so encumbered. It was a Catholic ceremony, in spite of everything, since his motives were understandable, and since the year was 2002, not 1802 (how I longed to have been born in the latter, earlier). In the open casket, his face was refreshingly clean-shaven, his eyes closed in supreme knowledge or ignorance. That was the Sunday night. Monday morning, in the green, in the open, in the dirt, with a lone hornet haunting and my underwear chafing, he was buried. He was buried in the silent city of Colma, while a hornet grew crazed on my pheromones.

ON THE morning of my father's burial, I sat on the edge of my parents' bed as my mother knotted my hair into a chignon, identical to the one she was wearing. After she had finished, she stood behind me in the mirror for a moment, hands resting on my shoulders, beauty a ghost of my own. I cast my eyes away while the impression was still fresh, before my glory could be undermined by that ancient guilt.

The funeral and subsequent reception were attended by a throng of professors, professors' wives, admiring grad students, and my popular mother's friends, who more than made up for our lack of living family. I moved about, dry-eyed yet downcast at my mother's side, accepting the hand-claspings, cheekbrushings, and misplaced compliments that came my way ("How tall and slim you've gotten! Like a model," "Doesn't Laurel look lovely in black?"). Out of sheer boredom, I kept coming back to the refreshments table for more cucumber sandwiches. I was nibbling on my third when I found my mother talking to Mr. and Mrs. Walden.

The Waldens were a middle-aged couple who had known my parents for almost twenty years. About ten years ago, they'd relocated to Carmel-by-the-Sea, an artsy little town down in Monterey County. Since then, my mother had been in touch with Jillian Walden only sporadically, calling her on the phone and lunching with the couple whenever they came up to the city. My father, busy with his professorly duties, preferred to forgo these meetings. Nonetheless, they had driven up expressly for his funeral, and extended their sympathies—Jillian, with brimming eyes, lamenting the terrible illness that had cut short poor Jonathon's life; Lee, with brusque joviality, stating, "Jon was a great guy. Really, he was great; a fine man."

"We're just sorry we can't stay longer," Jillian told us, "Lee's working to a deadline."

"Another English garden. They want hedge animals— squirrels, rabbits, the whole deal—but tell me it can't look *kitsch*."

"Oh, dear," my mother frowned in sympathy.

"Hedges are all he can talk about! He isn't very good company at the moment," Jillian laughed, "And, as for Josie, she spends all her time with the boyfriend. It doesn't matter that she won't be seeing us when she goes back to college. Laurel, do you have a boyfriend?" Mrs. Walden turned to me.

I shook my head and tried not to roll my eyes, giving her a polite simper. I had long since finished my sandwich. The women exchanged coy glances.

"Good for you. All Josie's man is good for is tracking sand in from the beach and stealing my beer," Lee griped.

"We make him stay in the guest room, of course," his wife added.

Lee gave a snort of derision. "Jill, you know as well as I do that that bed has never been slept on."

"It *is* a lovely room," Jillian continued, diplomatically. "We renovated it last winter. It's a shame for it to go unused. Josie's room will probably just sit empty for most of the year as well . . ." She glanced at her husband, who nodded. "Lee and I were talking on the way here: we'd love to have you and Laurel come to stay sometime! Carmel is beautiful in September—still sunny and warm. Perfect weather for you to paint in. And Laurel can swim."

"Oh! Jill, how nice of you!" My mother's brows went up in gratitude. "But we couldn't impose like that."

"Really, Lizzie, we wouldn't ask if we didn't mean it! We hardly get to see you anymore. And Laurel—you probably don't even remember ever coming to Carmel." Jillian swatted me gently on my bare arm.

"Oh . . . I do." I had to turn my attention away from the napkin that I had idly been folding and refolding to look at her. In fact, I did vaguely recall a weekend by the beach when I was eight or nine, and sharing a slant-ceilinged bedroom with their dark-haired daughter. I also recalled that I would be starting school again in three weeks' time. I informed the adults of this fact and there was a general murmur of disappointment.

"Of course, there's always Josie's old school," Jillian said, after a deliberative pause. "Boarding isn't for everyone, but we were very impressed by Saint Cecilia's. Their music program, I think, was what got her into Pomona."

"Great campus too. Built in the thirties. A bit Deco, a bit Gothic. You'd love the chapel, Lizzie." Lee shot my mother a glance, hooking his thumbs into his belt.

"I don't know if boarding school is the best thing for Laurel right now." My mother looked up at me. Once again, I was forced to rein in my wandering attention: this time, from a group of male professors who I'd been inspecting.

"It might be good for her to get away from all the grief. What do you think, sweetheart?" Jillian smiled at me. I gave her another simper.

"You should at least let us show you around the place. Wonderful stuff. Carvings, clerestories, willow trees. I think there's even a lake . . ."

"Don't forget the woods, dear," Jillian interrupted her husband. "Such beautiful woods!"

September 11, 2002

Saint Cecilia's Catholic School
Marin County

Dear Mom,

Everything is fine here. I like my new uniform better than the old one. We actually have proper kilts, and the emblem on my blouse (an eye and a harp, the same as on the letterhead) is really well stitched. There was a memorial assembly this morning, but we still had to go to classes. I couldn't be bothered playing hockey in P.E. though.

I hope that you are having a good time at Yellow Leaf. You deserve a break from things. Tell Lee and Jillian hello. I will be down at Thanksgiving to help with the house. Write soon.

Your daughter,

Laurel E. Marks

PART TWO

In many ways, my life only truly began on a day in September, when I was seventeen and far from everything. Before that day, life had been elsewhere; something utterly apart from me and the slanted sunbeams and wooden floors of my childhood. I like to think that I was born in those woods, in a flash of green and stream of sepia sunlight—the mythic haze of that Marin County Monday. Everything before that September day was simply a prelude, leading up to the shock of my conception: bereft, kneeling, as he stood like a god in my sunlight, his white shirt ablaze.

The tears that brought me to the woods were nothing. They were the strain of staring through a classroom window in the hour before lunch break. They were three weeks of pent-up grief and self-condemnation. They were an exacerbation of my fragile beauty, luring that god into the shadows of my arbor, where California laurel grew heady and tangled as a dream.

He was a god. His arms were strong, his shoulders broad. His manner was warm and paternal. He had hair on the back of his hands and a pale gold wedding band that flashed when he moved to console me. I didn't resist his embrace, but cried into his shirtfront—sweet, salt tears that mingled with the smell of his skin. He kneaded my shoulders. He stroked my hair. He murmured in my ear—smooth, hot-breathed nothings.

If it weren't for the bell, sounding over the school grounds to reach us in our leafy recess, our illicit embrace, he might have had me then, as any god would a nymph. As it was, we broke apart: I, with the sudden awareness of how old he was; he with the awareness of how young I was. He looked upon my innocent white blouse, my kilt and high white socks, with something akin to horror. I looked upon his collared shirt and sensible, belted trousers, and looked away in embarrassment. He didn't try to prevent me as I gathered my things and fled from that green inferno.

WHILE ENROLLING at Saint Cecilia's three weeks earlier, I had been obliged to make the usual selections among subjects. There were the sciences: biology, chemistry, and physics. There were the foreign languages: French, German, Spanish, Italian, and Mandarin. There were the mathematics: algebra, calculus, geometry, and statistics. Finally, there was English literature. At senior level, this was divided into three classes: Modernism, taught by Mr. Wolfstein; women's literature, taught by Mrs. Poplar; and Romantic poetry, taught by Mr. Steadman.

I had no real interest in the writings of women. Meanwhile, though only a month ago, the word "modern" would have held more appeal for me, my father's death had effected a change, which made me linger over the final option. I skimmed the reading list. My pen hovered above my page. I sighed and scribbled in my small, jerky hand: *Romantic poetry.*

After Monday's lunch hour, I arrived outside my fifth period art class, flustered and grass-stained, with a stray leaf in my hair. The leaf was pointed out to me by Jade van Dam—a slight, snooty girl with seed-like green eyes and bobbed brown hair—and subsequently plucked out by bold little Marcelle

Lavigne, who had been in my French lesson prior to lunch, and who wisecracked, "What have *you* been doing?" When the door to the art room was opened by Ms. Faber, I made a point to sit away from both girls at the communal table, taking a place beside fat Winnie Maddock, who obscured me from general view.

I passed from fifth period to study hall, study hall to dinner, dinner to dormitory, as if in a dream—granted, a very warm dream, invaded at times by hyper-real flashes of foliage, pearly buttons, and dark arm hair. I recognized these flashes as a different kind of reality, which had very little to do with eating or sleeping, or with buttoning my blouse, slow-fingered, in the still near-darkness of my private dorm room on Tuesday morning. Nor did it have anything to do with walking alongside Sadie Bridges, another senior, to check the beds of the younger girls under our charge and asking her whether she had biology class first period. "No, sorry, I take chem." She yawned into her palm.

I settled on my stool in the basement laboratory at nine A.M. for my biology lesson, dream unbroken, third row center. The class was conducted by Mr. Higginbottom, a gentle giant of a man with a jutting jaw, dressed in lumberjack plaid. Before all else, he informed us of his faith in Our Christian God, which in no way conflicted with his profession as a scientist. As I listened to him speaking slowly, earnestly, about the beauty of the natural world, intelligent design, I knew that his God had nothing to do with the flesh and blood god who had taken me into his arms the previous day, in a world of sun and trees and open air. For the rest of the lesson, I took to staring out the window, at the path to the library, which was lined with blurred red azaleas.

When the bell went, I rose, still dreaming. I had a long walk from the science wing to my first lesson in Romantic poetry, which was located on the top floor of the building that overlooked Trinity Catholic College, our brother school. Caught in the rush between classes, I moved with the crowd up three flights of stairs to the place where I took algebra, and across a bridge to the humanities wing. There, I missed my classroom, and was forced to turn back when I reached another bridge. This led down to the performing arts center, from which a clanging of musical instruments could already be heard. By the time that I arrived at the wooden door—windowless, carved with an Art Deco sunburst—of my English class, the lesson was already seemingly in progress. I quietly slid the door along its tracks—unfortunately, not quietly enough to enter the room undetected.

He wore chino pants, a cornflower blue shirt. He was holding the prop of an attendance list. All the same, there was no mistaking him for another man. He stared at me with a look of open astonishment, trailing off in the middle of roll call. I flamed. I faltered. I set my sights on an empty desk beside the window, and began my walk of shame across the room, ignoring a gleeful "*Psst!*" from Marcelle Lavigne.

Once I was seated, he seemed to recover himself, returning to the class list with admirable composure. He announced the names of my classmates in a clear, sonorous voice. When he got to my own, he paused, eyelashes fluttering down at the page. I could have sworn that a smile, tenderly suppressed, was already itching at the corners of his mouth. He raised his eyes to look me full in the face as he addressed me, "Laurel Marks?" I nodded and my own eyes flashed, as if I were hearing my name aloud for the first time ever.

I HAD never before had a teacher as eloquent as Mr. Steadman. I knew this within the first ten minutes of the lesson, in which he described to us what we could expect from his course. He would introduce us to the Romantic poets. He would discuss with us the nature of the sublime, love, freedom, and revolution. He would instruct us in the ways of the Byronic hero. All of this, he told us in the smoothest possible manner: smiling blithely and swaggering up to the blackboard, where he scrawled his notes left-handedly in illegible white chalk. All of this seemed calculated to seduce me, and me alone.

As I watched him, the possibility of a new, dynamic god, changeable yet cultivated, was made flesh before my eyes. He was not the abstract ectomorph that I was accustomed to, but expressive and robust, with hands that gestured widely as he spoke, and roving eyes that were not afraid to make contact; that seemed to seek it out, if anything. Though he didn't glance my way too frequently, the spellbinding flow of his movements and the perfection of his timing meant that I was utterly rapt when he did, and had no way of tearing my eyes from him. In fact, I couldn't even bring myself to look away long enough to discern whether he was having the same effect on the other girls. Instead, I sat back in my chair, focusing my attentions on perceiving every aspect of his bright, shifting divinity.

Even then, I might have analyzed it. Even then, I might have told myself that it was no coincidence that he was my father's age; that he stood an even six foot tall, as my father had; that his eyes and hair were dark, just as my father's had been. How little the analysis would have mattered though, when confronted with the brute desirability of the man at the front of the room, who was more solid, more tangibly male than my father ever had been; whose dark eyes were quick and hot, like liquid fire; who was getting enthusiastic, very enthusiastic, about the sublime. In his resonant voice, he read us passages from Burke, speaking of the masculine properties of size, strength, and turbulence, and the passion of terror these properties inspired; a passion, he assured us, which had its origins in our fear of death.

When the bell went and my classmates stood up from their seats, I stayed sitting for another heartbeat, stunned. It was as if my mind had been plundered of all its contents. "Tomorrow we look at Wordsworth. I may bring in some daffodils," he finished with levity, closing the book from which he had been expounding. I noticed that the room was rapidly emptying. I rose from my own chair, crossing to the door. He was heading in the same direction. He stopped at the doorway to let me pass before him, nodding my name. "Laurel." I thanked him and hurried ahead, eyes averted.

Upon leaving the room, my heart skipping, I found myself face-to-face once again with Marcelle, the girl from my art class. She was standing with two friends, looking exceedingly short in her long socks, with her heavy-duty ring binder pressed against her chest. "Hey, new girl," she called out to me brashly, as I attempted to make a beeline for the bathroom. Steadman passed with a high head and a leather briefcase, suddenly incognito, on his way to the teachers' lounge. "What's-your-name, Lauren? You're in my art class, aren't you? And my French. Amanda does French too." Marcelle gestured toward a busty, brassy blonde of about my height, who came forward. Her other friend Graziella hung back in the shadows by the lockers, dumpy and shrewish.

"I remember *you*," Amanda said with a simper, "You ran off so quickly after class yesterday. We didn't get a chance to introduce ourselves. Where were you going?"

"Oh . . ." I saw tears, blurred leaves, Steadman. "I had some enrollment stuff to take care of."

"Where are you from?" she persisted.

"Convent of the Sacred Heart."

"Come downstairs with us!" Marcelle interjected, linking her arm with mine.

It was in this manner that I found myself being pulled along by Marcelle: a forceful girl, though at least a head shorter than I was. She had fine, almost whitish hair and cartoonish features: convex forehead, protuberant gray eyes, ski-slope nose. Alongside me, she skipped and clowned, tripping over the laces of her oxfords and cursing her own clumsiness. "*Merde!*"

"Marcy, you dope," Amanda jeered behind us. Tall, ripe, and amber-eyed, Amanda moved with hip-swaying slowness. Alongside her, Graziella shuffled in silence.

We descended to the ground floor and sat ourselves down on a patch of lawn, which looked out over a sunny area of benches, coffee carts, and stainless-steel bubblers. Graziella left us to buy a cinnamon bun. In her absence, Amanda widened her eyes and told me in an aside, "That girl is *such* a bore lately. She broke up with her boyfriend over the summer."

"And fat lately," Marcelle giggled, taking a box of Good & Plentys from her bag and offering them around. Naturally, I refused.

"Yes! She wasn't always that fat," Amanda cooed excitedly. She gestured across the lawn. "See that girl over there, the super trampy one? That one with mahogany hair and her skirt up to here?" Amanda raised her hands to an improbably high place near her crotch. "Gratzi used to be her size last year."

"Not Siobhan," Marcelle protested, vehemently chewing her candy. "She was never as skinny as Siobhan."

They continued arguing about their girlfriend's former dimensions until she returned, eating her thickly iced bun. "We were just saying how pretty Dana Nissen would be if she got her skin fixed," Amanda covered her tracks, inviting Graziella to sit down again. The girl made a noise of assent between mouthfuls and plumped herself down on the grass.

I only half-listened as Amanda continued pointing out other girls in the area: "that freak Mitzi" who slouched and never spoke; the two lesbians, Ella Massie and Cassidy Park, who were not, contrary to appearances, an item; the trio of beauties, Jade van Dam, Jessica Britton, and Kaitlin Pritchard—all of whom were student committee girls and "total Christians," according to Amanda. Having accorded me this information, she stopped and looked at me expectantly, her amber eyes as clear and cold as a hawk's. It took me a moment to realize that she'd asked me a question, and another moment to realize that I was under no obligation to tell the truth about myself.

"My parents are getting a divorce," I began. "Dad's gone to work in Germany until it's finalized and Mom's staying with friends. They still don't know what to do with the house. I'll probably be spending Christmas in Trier . . ."

THE NEXT day, I was far more prepared for his lesson, having primped in the mirror beforehand and found a friend to sit with. Marcelle had helped herself to my window seat. I settled for the aisle, an arm's length away from Amanda, who maintained her place in the front-center row with Graziella. To my annoyance, Marcelle kept leaning across me during the lesson to get at her friends in the next row, blocking my view of Steadman.

That Wednesday, Mr. Steadman had dressed himself in a pale striped shirt, worn with a silky tie of swirled gold and brown paisley and the beige chinos of the day before. The promised daffodils were in a vase on his desk, dazzling and yellow. He smiled through roll call, taking sips from a mug of coffee that he'd brought with him straight from morning break. He had also brought along some printouts, which he set about distributing, starting from our desk. We had the best desk in the whole classroom, by the window and right next to his own.

"Would you care to hand these back, girls?" Mr. Steadman said, passing the papers to Marcelle and me, and charming us with a look that made me blush and her yip with laughter.

Thick brows. Molten black eyes. Roman nose. Dangerous sickle of a smile, sending cold thrills down my spine, hot flutters through my stomach. I tried to find fault with him, I did. His teeth were imperfect. His waistline was thicker than it could have been. There were a few wrinkles at the corners of his mouth and eyes. The more I looked, however, the more his faults seemed like perfections. His wrinkles were lines of expression, adding to the imperfect charm of his sharp canines and slightly crooked incisors. The spare weight around his middle only made him seem more loveable, more lavish with his affections, as well as more appetitive and therefore likely to succumb to my affections. Moreover, it didn't prevent him from being an incredibly well-proportioned man, with broad shoulders, long limbs, and strong, sinewy forearms.

It was a lesson of Wordsworth, the Lake District. Our desk by the window, overlooking the lake and the weeping willows. As Steadman spoke to us about the glittering blue waters, the green fells and golden daffodils that inspired Wordsworth and his likes, Marcelle nudged me in the ribs, drew my attention to the view outside the window. Some rowers were pushing off from the banks, sweeping across the water in crews of four. "Trinity boys!" she mouthed. She leaned across me and made the same remark to Amanda, who gasped and asked "Is Seamus there?" Marcelle squinted, whispered "I think so." Amanda simpered and patted her hair with the back of her hand.

"Girls," Steadman warned us, good-humoredly.

I straightened up and met his eye, wanting desperately to show him that I wasn't interested in the view outside, in anything beyond that room. I was perhaps too attentive, too rigid in my posture and intent in my gaze—that is, as long as the lesson lasted. As soon as the lesson was over, I was quick to lower my eyes. I didn't dare look at him as he stood by the door to let me pass, to let all of us pass before him. Nevertheless, I did keep my ears sharpened to his warm, murmured farewells, even as my friends ran their mouths off.

"You have to come see the boys with us," Marcelle was saying to me, "and tell us who you think is hotter."

"Seamus, of course," Amanda swanned ahead of us, a load of books pressed to her overdeveloped chest.

"No, Flynn."

"Seamus."

". . . Amanda . . . Marcelle . . ." Steadman beamed down at my friends from the threshold. "Laurel. Until tomorrow . . ."

After Wednesday's English class, I had gym, where I was free to strip off my clothes while his presence was still fresh on my mind. In the locker room, I undressed, like all the other pretty girls, out in the open. I had never felt more refreshed by the sight of my small breasts in their white lace bra, my flat stomach, my jutting hips, than after that lesson with Mr. Steadman. I cast what I hoped was a cool eye over the bodies in my vicinity, though my heart was still beating rapidly, my hands fumbling as I dressed myself in the bright red shorts and T-shirt of my gym uniform.

The class consisted of fourteen girls in identical red costumes, wielding hockey sticks as silver-haired Ms. Da Silva looked on. Legs and buttocks. Bouncing busts. My own swinging ponytail and slow trot, which dwindled to a sedate stroll, eventually coming to a standstill. I had never been one for physical activity and was content to linger on the fringes of the game. Four or five other girls did the same, gossiping and fanning away flies.

As much as I strained to, I really had no hope of seeing into his classroom from the playing field. His classroom faced east over the lake and willows and was separated from the athletic fields by a quarter mile of shrubbery, a parking lot, a mowed lawn, and the curves of the performing arts center. It was pure fancy to think that he could see me, barelegged, clad in red; to imagine that his breath, and not the humidity, was responsible for the hair tickling my nape. I sighed. I struck the head of my hockey stick against the ground and dug it into the turf.

I was a warm, clear Friday and no Trinity boys were in sight. He led us down to the lake for our lesson, last period of the day, carrying a crate of books and dressed in a tweed suit. As we were leaving the English department, he greeted fat Mrs. Poplar, who was in a hurry and fanning herself with a printout, and was greeted by twenty-six-year-old Miss Kelsen, who I hated on sight for her sweet blue gaze, dimples, and pert ass (but who, I later heard, was thankfully engaged to the rowing instructor at Trinity).

We collapsed in the shade of the willows, legs splayed out, faces turned up to the sun. Without being told to, we had formed a loose circle: the twelve of us sitting, him standing at the head. He seemed taller and trimmer in his tweed suit, with the crisp white shirt underneath. His hair was boyishly floppy with two dark, hanging forelocks. He placed the crate of books at his feet, with the words, "Page ninety-six, Cambridge and the Alps."

I brushed my hair from my face, leaning forward to take a volume and briefly arresting his gaze, before settling back on my haunches. I was crouching almost directly across from him, a position ideal for watching his face as he recited—though I couldn't help envying the girls who flanked him. He had seated himself casually with his legs apart, arm dangling from a raised knee, and bookmarked the Wordsworth with his index finger. Once we each had a copy open on our tartan laps, he flipped back to the page effortlessly and began to read aloud in his clearest, most sonorous voice.

I knew already that he was a man of extraordinary eloquence, from our lessons earlier in the week. Still, to hear his flow of words unbroken, over the course of a leisurely hour, was something else. I was at leisure, not only to look and listen, but to love and be lulled by his smoothness, by the play of light and shadow of his features, and the solidity of his presence. I was lulled into a trance of adoration, which showed through the slackening of my posture, the sprawl of my limbs, the fingers tugging and caressing at the grass with unwarranted urgency. An observer may have said that his body, positioned across from mine with legs spread, was subtly addressing itself toward me. Although little eye contact took place, our loins were in alignment; the air buzzed between us. My fingers were sensitive to all stimulation, roaming across the grass to the hem of my skirt and through my hair.

I wasn't the only girl who showed signs of being affected by his articulacy. There wasn't one among us who didn't appear relaxed—though there was an ambiguity, in some cases, as to whether the drooping bodies and lobotomized expressions were the product of enchantment or utter boredom. Many seemed half-asleep, reclining on the grass or leaning on their friends for support. Marcelle, I saw, was biting her thumb, while Emma

Smith had her head in Karen Harmsworth's lap. The heat, combined with the dullness of the poetry, the soothing resonance of Steadman's voice and the distraction of being outdoors, seemed to have produced in all of us a perverse dreaminess, which expressed itself as an enhanced physicality. Enchanted or not, there was no doubt in my mind that he had brought us there as his attendant nymphs. Until the hour was up, he would be our patron god.

The hour had to be up at some point, though I was unprepared for it happening while the sun was still out and his lips still moving. I was admiring, yet again, the prominence of his cheekbones, the downward point of his Roman nose, and the shadow on his upper lip from where he had shaved. With his jacket on, I was prevented from appreciating the sinewy, golden-haired forearms; instead, taking in the breadth of his shoulders, the wide-open legs and, more importantly, the crotch. In the presence of such virility, it was impossible not to imagine that I knew how it all worked; that I was ready for it, virginity aside. I adjusted my limbs. The willows bristled. The lake was wide, receptive, taking on their green.

A moment later, it was over. I looked down at the pages of my book without comprehending what had happened, why he had stopped. He thanked us for our patience, told us that he looked forward to seeing us again the following week. We were instructed to pass the books back his way. I relinquished mine with difficulty. As we rose from the grass, brushing off our kilts and stretching languorously, the end-of-day bell sounded. He hoisted up the crate of books, scanning our faces with embarrassing eagerness. "Does anyone want to help me carry these upstairs? Anyone. . . ?"

Our eyes met briefly over the others' heads. My heart leapt at the opportunity. I looked away, swallowing my desire. I knew I regretted my decision a moment later, as I shouldered my satchel and followed my friends uphill. By the time that I cast a glance back in the direction of his beloved, tweed-clad form, I saw that he was already some distance away; that I'd given up my only chance of being alone with him again that week.

MORNING BROUGHT with it a loathing for daylight, the stale smell of the pillowcase against my nose. I closed my eyes and occupied myself for a few minutes longer in the warm dimness beneath my lids. We were standing by the lake. He had singled me out to help him carry the books. I assented. I ascended with him, up two flights of stairs to the dusty storeroom. He took the load from my arms. He locked the door behind us. He pressed me into a corner and began to unbutton my blouse: slowly, expertly . . .

There were giggles outside my dorm, a stifled knock. I had made a late-morning date with the others: takeaway coffee and a walk to the Trinity campus to scope out the boys. I wondered whether they would leave me alone if I ignored them for long enough; realizing, however, that my train of fantasy had been broken, and that I had nothing else to do that day, I decided to get up. I opened the door to find them standing in the frame, brassy blonde and white blonde, dressed almost identically in denim skirts and low-cut, flutter-sleeved blouses. "You're *still* in your nightie?" Amanda sneered.

"Sorry, I slept in." I let them into my tiny room, hoping they couldn't smell my fingertips. I went to my wardrobe, where I knew I had a white blouse—albeit, with a prim, lacy collar instead of a plunging V-neck. In the absence of denim, I chose a plain black skirt to go with it. "Just give me a minute in the bathroom to change."

"Change here. We don't care," Amanda said dismissively.

"We promise we won't perv!" Marcelle covered her eyes in demonstration, then uncovered them, catching sight of something she liked in my wardrobe. "Oh, look, Mandy! This is just like that dress I wanted to buy in San Rafael last year."

Amanda sidled closer. "You have some cute things."

I left them there, skulking across to the other side of my room to change. It dawned on me that I'd have to forgo fresh underwear, at least for the morning. When I was dressed, I began working on my hair, which sleep had tangled into a dense auburn thicket. My face in the mirror was as unmade as my bed, but not unpretty. "I'm ready," I turned to them.

"Finally," Amanda heaved a sigh, more huffily than was necessary. "Come on. I'll just *die* if I don't get to see Seamus today."

OUTSIDE, THE Saint Cecilia's grounds were bustling with girls out of uniform, heading to their Saturday-morning extracurriculars, escorting visitors around campus, or simply loafing about on sunny lawns and around the shopping precinct. Sipping from paper cups, the three of us crossed through the vacant foreign languages department and made toward the lake where we'd been less than a day before with Steadman. My heart leapt. I glanced back at the school building and tried to identify his classroom from the rows of arched windows on the upper floor.

It was a half-hour walk from our side of the lake to the heart of Trinity Catholic College. Along the way, they pointed out an old building to me, boasting the ballroom where Homecoming, Winterfest, and other such events typically took place. "Homecoming is in the first week of October," Amanda informed me. "You can only go if you've got a date, but don't worry—we'll get you one."

Constructed a few decades before Saint Cecilia's, the boys' school was, according to Lee Walden, "Pure Collegiate Gothic." Boys got about on bikes or loped along with gym bags, occasionally turning their heads at the group of us—though most of them, evidently, had somewhere else to be. When we reached the central plaza, however, with its low steps and decorative fountain, I was struck by the sheer number of boys in the area and how magnetically their eyes seemed to be drawn to our faces, chests, and legs. Suddenly, I felt exposed in my short, black skirt. "Of course, Siobhan and Hannah are right by the fountain," Amanda said hypocritically, "They're practically *begging* to get their T-shirts wet."

"Look! Look! Tracey is talking to James Pemberton." Marcelle waved gleefully across the plaza, "Trace-*yyy*! Hi-*ii*!"

"Shut up, Marcy. You're going to get us kicked out."

"Kicked out?" I ventured, timidly.

"Well, *technically*, we're not supposed to be here without a visitor's pass," Amanda explained. "Really, we'll be fine, as long as Marcy stops screaming and we stand off to the side somewhere. What about those trees there?" Without waiting for our approval, the busty Queen Bee led us into the shade beneath some yellow-green maples to the side of the plaza.

"Make sure you tell us if you see someone you like, Laurel."

At Amanda's behest, I cast my eyes over the smorgasbord of young males in the vicinity, attempting to control my underenthusiasm. Flat-bellied. Spotted. Smooth-cheeked or, worse still, sporting pathetic pubic down. Every one of them lacking in the sublime qualities that made a man. Though my expression was hardly encouraging, my indifferently wandering eye seemed to be enough to make one boy nudge another. After a moment of conspiring, the pair were swaggering toward us: both tall, lean, brown-haired, unremarkable. "That's Roy Chalmers, and that's—oh, hi, Larry."

"Mandy, Marcelle." They grinned and nodded. Then, one of the boys—not the one whose eye I had caught, but the other—addressed me politely. "I'm afraid I don't know your name."

"She's our German friend!" Marcelle lied, laughing ecstatically.

"*Guten tag,*" the eye-catcher said flirtatiously, with a solemn incline of his head. I glanced away, embarrassed for him. The other gave a Hitler salute, causing my friends to erupt into giggles.

"She isn't really. She's from Sacred Heart," Amanda elaborated, once their laughter had died down. Before they could ask anything else about me, she changed the subject. "Hey, have either of you seen Seamus Head?"

"Who's asking?" the saluter responded. He received a playful wallop.

"If you want, we can tell him you were looking for him," my admirer offered.

"We'll tell him you were *desperate* to find him . . ."

"Yes, tell him!" Marcelle nodded fervently.

"Shut up, Marcy," Amanda scowled, "and Roy, don't you dare. I just want to ask him if he's signing up for Model Congress again this year."

Across the plaza, Hannah Williams let out a squeal as one of the boys by the fountain attacked her with a spray of water. A grim-faced Trinity worker, some kind of groundskeeper or guard, emerged from behind the fountain and, with dark looks, sent Hannah and Siobhan packing. He began stalking across the plaza, toward our maple grove. "Oh, *merde,*" said Amanda. "Sorry, guys. We have to go."

WE LEFT Trinity the same way that we'd come, avoiding trouble by taking the rapid downhill path to the athletic fields. The only adult we saw between there and the plaza was a small, worn woman, walking two boys who seemed far too young to be of Trinity age. "Good morning, Mrs. H.!" Marcelle greeted her, as we passed her by outside the basketball courts. Mistrustfully, the mother looked up, then went back to wiping a snotty nose.

"Mr. Higginbottom's wife," Amanda explained. "It's disgusting how many children they have."

Marcelle disagreed: "When I'm married, I want a hundred babies!"

"Maybe you should ask Mr. H. if he wants a second wife," Amanda said, provoking Marcelle into a fit of scandalized giggles.

The lake came into sight: a smudge of dark blue-gray beyond the gym and rowing shed. As luck would have it, three young males with overdeveloped deltoids, dressed in sweat-pitted tank tops, were filing out of the gymnasium. They spied us. They conferred briefly among themselves and, in a matter of seconds, were upon us. One of them swept Marcelle up in his arms, swinging her around, before passing her onto a friend, who did the same thing. Meanwhile, another boy—Seamus, presumably—was advancing on Amanda, attempting to cover her face with his stinking armpit. Both girls squealed in protest.

Suddenly as they had come, the young men were off. "Where are you going?" Amanda called after her beau. "Lunch," he grinned over his shoulder. She stared after them, arms akimbo. Marcelle lay panting on the grass, where the boys had set her down, her denim skirt raised to her crotch.

FOR ALL their antics, my friends were busy girls, with extra-curriculars to occupy them in the hours between lunch and dinner. Amanda left with dull Graziella for clarinet practice; soon after, Marcelle went to her flute lesson, to be followed by an hour and a half of drama. Finally, divinely alone, I walked the red-azalea path to the library and borrowed a volume of Wordsworth, which I took along with me into the woods.

My laurel trees were just as they had been on Monday, listing toward one another, a shady and aromatic arbor. They grew among live oak, big-leaf maples, Pacific madrone, on the outer limits of the forest. In this part of the woods, there was still sunlight to be seen, falling in narrow, dusty beams through the canopy. I nestled into place between the two trunks and turned to the first page of *The Prelude*.

> *Oh there is blessing in this gentle breeze*
> *A visitant that while it fans my cheek*
> *Doth seem half-conscious of the joy it brings . . .*

At what point I set my book down, and abandoned myself fully to the heady scent of the leaves, the heady thoughts I had gone there to entertain, I don't know. Suffice it to say, I remembered little of what I read that day.

DOUBLE MATH on Monday mornings was a painful way to begin a week, if there ever was one. I had no friends in Mr. Slawinski's math class, so was alone when I emerged back into the hallway at morning break, fuzzy-headed from too much algebra. On a whim, I decided to visit the English department.

I crossed to the humanities wing just in time to see Mr. Steadman's blue-shirted back disappearing into the faculty lounge. The effect this had on me was entirely disproportionate, as I found myself beaming into the distance, long after he'd gone inside. A whack in the side from somebody's satchel was what brought me out of my daydream. I moved along, only to spy an empty locker one classroom down from his.

I can't overstate the important role that locker played for me over the following weeks. It was because of that locker that I was free to visit his department as often as I wished, even on Mondays, when my timetable was sadly Steadman-free. That day alone, I must have passed by his classroom four or five times. The movement aroused little suspicion, though Marcelle did furrow her brow when she came with me to dispatch some books before art class that afternoon. "I don't remember your locker being up here."

It was because of the locker that I came to know his timetable: to witness the ninth-graders lining up outside his room, as I collected my textbook for history on the floor below with Mr. Henderson; to slam the door and press my *Trésors du Temps* to my chest, arming myself for when I'd see him pass by, carrying a crate of books to his juniors. When I had math, gym, and biology, however, his room was always empty: the door open and the ceiling lights illuminating his absence.

I was purposefully forgetful, prancing off to French class with Amanda and Marcelle, then cursing myself ("*merde!*") and telling them I'd once again forgotten my homework, my dictionary. It didn't matter that I was earning myself a reputation for absentmindedness—the extra glimpse of him was worth it. Sometimes, passing each other in the hall, I would get more than a glimpse. Our eyes would meet and, for that brief moment, I knew that he saw me, that I was in his thoughts, whether he admitted it or not. Once or twice, a greeting was attempted, but this never worked out well. His mouth formed the words and my head jerked away, in what was meant to be a nod but looked more like a gesture of avoidance.

When walking with my friends, I ignored him entirely. I hoped to convey an aura of mystery and inaccessibility, as well as conforming to the accepted etiquette between teachers and students outside of class hours. No matter how well liked he was in the classroom, in the hallways he became invisible, as every other adult was, among the throngs of uniformed girls. There were some exceptions to these rules, but I didn't understand them; didn't understand how some could skip up to their favorite teachers and start conversing, right there in the open. I was distressed one day to witness from afar beautiful Kaitlin Pritchard, with her hair loose, talking to Mr. Steadman outside the English department. She was holding a box and shifting her weight from foot to foot; he was leaning close and, even from that distance, I could tell that he was laughing, enjoying her shiny presence. Did she know him, I wondered, or did she simply know, with the confidence of a girl much prettier than myself, how to charm him? I turned over both possibilities in my mind, unsure of which depressed me more.

I HAD questioned my friends about Steadman with little success, receiving only the vaguest replies when I asked them what they thought of the tall, dark, forty-something-year-old charmer who taught us Romantic poetry. "He's okay, maybe a bit weird," Amanda and Marcelle answered in more or less the same terms. "Why weird?" I tried not to look offended. "Oh, you know, the way that he goes on about things," Amanda said. "Like he's trying to show off how much he knows," Marcelle added.

I convinced myself not to take this judgment to heart. All teachers were weird, when I thought about it. Six-foot-seven Mr. Higginbottom was weird with his plaid shirts, sermons, and brood of seven boys. Five-foot-six Mr. Slawinski was weird with his cold-blue gaze, shaved head, and immunity to the charms of pretty girls when they tried to flirt their way out of bad test scores or forgotten math homework. Madame Rampling, the francophile Englishwoman who taught us French, was weird. Mr. Henderson, who wore shorts and gartered socks in all weathers, as if his hairy hams were too attractive to cover up, was weird. Mr. Wolfstein, the head of the English department, was weird with his turtlenecks, tobacco-scented beard, and smoking breaks that lasted up to half a lesson. Marcelle and Amanda, who had been in his class the year earlier, still doubled over in mirth when they remembered the way that he used to sing poems instead of simply reciting them.

I took it upon myself to find out everything I could about Mr. Steadman. Every day, I watched and listened for new information. It was a fine Thursday when Mrs. Poplar knocked on the door of our classroom and asked him, in her simpering, middle-aged way, "Hugh, may I borrow you for a minute? I have a man's job for you in the next room." This was how I discovered his first name: Hugh.

Name: Hugh Steadman. Date of birth: February 29, 1960. I had learned as much a lesson earlier, listening to an exchange between him and Christina Tucci, who was bragging about having just turned eighteen. "Well, that makes you eight years older than I am! I've only had ten birthdays, you know" (a corny joke that I didn't really approve of, but that allowed me to calculate his true age, and the twenty-five years that lay between us).

I was not hurt by his casual habit of mentioning his wife in anecdotes. In fact, I already felt that I knew "Danielle." His twin children had also become familiar to me: sulky Cole and dutiful Catherine, who attended the same coed middle school. It seemed almost perverse that I should know anything about them—I, who had so many impure thoughts about their father. Although it would've made more sense to interpret such references as evidence of his love for them, I turned them to my own advantage: as I saw it, he was catering to *me*, indulging *my* curiosity, at the expense of their privacy.

I saw further evidence of indulgence in his approach to teaching, which encouraged rapt listening over reading and note-taking. On the rare occasions when he did assign us work during class, he would prowl the room with his hands in his pockets, moving between the desks with a swish of corduroy or chino cloth. Once a suitable amount of time had elapsed, he would come and crouch by our desks, looking over our shoulders at the skimming of eyes under fluttering lashes, or the scratching away of mechanical pencils. "That's an interesting point," he would murmur with a smile, or "What do you make of that couplet, there?" (pointing to the line in question with a hardy index finger, which I instantly imagined being touched by).

He was an indulgent teacher. He joked with his outgoing pupils and was kind and courtly with his timid ones, so that he seemed to favor anyone he spoke to. It was an honor to be the focus of such tact, such charisma—especially as I felt myself to be sorely lacking in both. If I imagined that he was more tender, more attentive with me than the others, however, I doubted it a moment later: listening to him lower his voice with shy Sally Flores, who sat alone in the row behind us, or conversing in Italian with Graziella and Christina on the other side of the room.

He knew Italian. Where he had learned it, I didn't know. I did know, for he had mentioned so in passing, that he had briefly attended the Perelman School of Medicine, dropping out after a year or so to study literature. I had the notion that his wife was also a doctor; that they had met while only students. This was confirmed a fortnight later when I heard that Kaitlin Pritchard had become chummy with Dr. Danielle

Steadman while volunteering at the children's hospital the year before, had even been invited over for dinner. I would have given anything to hear her describe the interior of their home, the manners of the lady of the house, and whether the handsome schoolmaster had made a pass at her while driving back to boarding school that night, but couldn't think of a polite way of asking.

The most trivial details of his life excited me. The mugs of milky coffee that he brought back from morning break and nursed, lukewarm, until lunch hour. The flowers that presided over the anarchy of his desk, larkspur and narcissus, plucked from his very own garden. His singular, left-handed scrawl, indecipherable in red ink, hopeless in white chalk. The outfits, teachers' outfits, paraded before me day after day.

There were beige chinos, cornflower shirt. Beige chinos, navy sweater-vest. Tweed suit, white shirt. White shirt, camel corduroys. Navy sport coat, slung over the back of his chair. On cooler days, he sometimes sported a sweater over his shirt and tie in charcoal, burgundy, or chocolate brown. Around the end of the month, he acquired a pair of gray herringbone trousers. Ties came in maroon, royal blue, gold and brown, patterned with paisley, fleur-de-lis, lozenges, and prancing Flemish lions. He wore brown wingtips, carried a brown leather briefcase. His wristwatch had a brown band and golden fixtures.

I had little desire to see him dressed otherwise. His buttons and buckles, his collars and cuffs, his taupe trouser socks, all filled me with a sweet, bright admiration. The desire to see him undressed was something else entirely: it was a desire that was almost too physical to entertain. Now and then, thinking more innocent thoughts, I would be assailed by images of dark, curled hair and tumescent flesh, never-before-seen flesh that, nevertheless, throbbed with heat and reeked of male sweat. It was all that I could do to keep myself from crying out

with the thought, which was less thought than sensation—
a brute, black force that made my knees clamp together, my
mind close shut.

My case wasn't helped by the fact that there were reminders
of him everywhere. The Molière play that we read for French
class, in which a man of forty-two plotted to marry his ward, a
girl of seventeen. Headlines over breakfast: a history teacher in
Vermont; a music teacher in Kentucky. The sight of the other
English teachers, alone: grizzled Mr. Wolfstein; fat Mrs. Poplar;
even that detested hussy, Miss Kelsen.

He was sociable, oh so sociable. I had seen him bounding
alongside Mr. Wolfstein, an excited pup next to the wolfish old
man. He was adored and caressed by Mrs. Poplar, a fond and
frumpy mother who, when I thought about it, couldn't have
been more than five years his senior. Naturally, he was flirta-
tious with Miss Kelsen. Yet as bitterly as I looked upon the
young woman's dimpled laughter, the older man's murmured
quips and upturned, explanatory palms, I was aware of his ways.
He was an incurable flirt.

He flirted with seniors, juniors, sophomores, freshmen;
with female teachers and librarians. Outside of work, I was
sure he was the sort of man who struck up conversations with
waitresses, shop girls, and stray women whom he saw waiting at
bus stops or on park benches. One art lesson, while burrowing
in the supplies closet for pastels, I was startled from my task by
what sounded like his sonorous voice blustering into the room.
"Flowers for milady," he greeted Ms. Faber, a snaggle-toothed
woman with a flesh-colored mole on her left cheek. I wasn't
thinking about her appearance then, however; the shock of his

voice had brought on graver concerns, as I sent the entire tin of pastels (located at last) crashing down, along with various brushes, twigs, hard erasers, and the good willow charcoals.

"Jeez, Laurel, stop dropping things!" Marcelle cackled across the room.

I bent down demurely to clear up the mess, aided by a couple of nearby handmaids. He didn't come to my service, but stayed standing with Ms. Faber, arms crossed and smiling (smirking?) at the proceedings. He was wearing his corduroys with the chocolate brown sweater, which brought out the chestnut tones in his hair. On my down-headed walk back to the communal table, I saw that he had placed a vase of amaryllises on Ms. Faber's desk.

Sitting down, I didn't look at him—simply smiled at Marcelle's jibes and piled my hair up, sticking it in place with a pencil. He continued speaking to Ms. Faber, asking if she knew the myth of Amaryllis, the white-clad girl who had stabbed herself repeatedly in the heart to make a bloody flower for her beloved. "Do we have English today, sir?" Marcelle interrupted. We did.

Ms. Faber thanked him for the flowers, which we were to begin drawing that lesson. It seemed nothing more would pass between us. On his way out of the studio, however, Mr. Steadman stooped by my desk, retrieving something from the speckled vinyl floor. "You'll be needing this," he smiled slyly, placing a red pastel before me.

It would be interesting to linger for a while in the art studio, a spacious annex of paneled windows and cool, northern light. It would be interesting to linger over the flowers drawn by each girl, the deviations of mind and body that they suggested.

Marcelle's flower, for instance, was clear and bright, some-what one-dimensional. Jade van Dam's was green-seeded, green-centered, in grading shades of pink rather than true red: intricate yet dispassionate. Winifred Maddock's was huge, shapeless, and somehow sad: the overblown bloom of a corpulent, side-burned virgin.

As for mine: raw and hungry and beginning to wilt, with petals that opened wide, only to turn back in on themselves. By the time that I completed enough drafts to transfer the thing to canvas, the outer white had diminished to an irregular fringe and the wilting had increased dramatically. The final product was, according to Ms. Faber, "expressionistic," full of pathos and lacking in perspective.

OUR DAYS in the sun were numbered. I knew it and, if the addi-tions to Mr. Steadman's wardrobe were anything to go by, he did too. Nevertheless, until mid-October, we were still having Fridays outdoors: a pleasure that he reserved for his seniors.

There was something traumatic about the beauty of those Fridays in the sunlight, where we could not touch. Sometimes under the enchantment of his words, I would let my legs open a little wider than I should have, in hope of enchanting him with a glimpse. I didn't know how much he saw, if indeed he ever looked (facing me across the circle, could he have avoided doing so?), yet no amount of shadowy thigh could have been an accurate measure of what I felt for him. My whole body could not have been an accurate measure. What I wanted was to merge with the grass, to be there under his fingertips, every nerve laid bare.

In the sunlight, however, I was untouchable, as was he. I knew this when I saw him closing his book, but also when I saw him laughing, joking with the other girls. One Friday, I even saw him stand up from the grass, to stretch and skim a stone across the glittering surface of the lake. Never again did he ask if anyone wanted to help him carry the books upstairs. Never again did he put himself within my reach.

Every Friday brought with it a new defeat, a new cup of sorrows. It got to the point where I couldn't even sit through Thursday's lesson without a certain awful fluttering in my stomach, a tightness in my chest, which was a premonition of the loss that I was to suffer the next day. The tweed suit became an object of ambivalence. Not to mention the willows, which caused me to fill whole pages of my notebook as follows:

I watch the willows weep and cannot breathe
I watch the willows weep and cannot breathe
I watch the willows weep and cannot breathe

It was the closest that I ever came to versifying my love, though now and again the instinct to express myself in words seemed to grab me by the throat. More than once, I had to stop myself from taking up a pen and making a journal entry in one of my notebooks; emotional expression was for the weak and, besides that, far too risky. I didn't even consider confessing my predicament to another girl, although I often longed for an ally—a perverse nurse or fairy godmother who would conspire with me to administer him love potions, and kindly lead me to the slaughter.

I had no illusions about my friendships with Marcelle and Amanda. Had I been less shadowy, more open about my aberrations, I might have dispensed with them entirely. As it was, I didn't have the courage for that; I required a cloak of conventionality. It had been the same before Steadman, when I was a student at Sacred Heart—though as my attendance became poorer and my eating habits more abstemious, the cloak began to slip. Sometimes, I wondered whether I would not be happier forming ties with a different variety of girls: girls who were not so shallow; who weren't constantly clowning and gossip-mongering; whose IQs weren't so much lower than my own. Casting my eye across the school grounds, however, the girls who attracted me weren't the solemn ones, but the shiny ones: the Jessica Brittons, Kaitlin Pritchards, and Jade van Dams of the world.

These girls would've sensed in a heartbeat that I didn't belong among them. It wasn't only that my GPA was lower than theirs, or that I had an aversion to committees, club memberships, and charitable pursuits. There was also that other thing—the shifty aspect of my admiration, which made me vie for the seat behind Kaitlin in history class, or a position near Jessica in the locker room, where I could get a good view of the hooks of her bra, the curve of her waist, the brown ponytail dangling between her shoulder blades.

I didn't respect my friends. I maintained a discreet distance between myself and them. Nevertheless, there were times when the intrusiveness I hated them for gave me to celebrate. I'm thinking of that Friday in the sunlight, when Marcelle sat herself beside me and, with childish admiration, began playing with my loose hair—winding it up and fanning it out and holding it up to the light. "Your hair is so pretty, Laurel," she told me guilelessly, as he stood nearby. My heart practically burst with gratitude. There was also another time, in the middle of a quiet English lesson, when Amanda leaned across the row to tell me in a cool stage whisper, "Lawrence Benning wants to date you."

"Lawrence Benning wants to *do* you," Marcelle echoed, at my other side.

"I don't know who that is," I said truthfully.

"You met him."

"Two weekends ago."

"I don't remember." I bit my lip and looked over at Steadman, who was working at his desk, a matter of feet away, feigning disinterest.

"Well, he wants you."

"Well . . ." I let the word hang in the air, a dreamy suggestion, as I continued to eye my only love, whose shirtsleeves were rolled up, whose brows were lowered, who wore a petulant pout of concentration. ". . . I don't care."

Later that lesson, Steadman came by with the mini essays that he had ostensibly been marking. "Beautiful, Laurel." His dark eyes met mine, as he passed back the meaningless slip of paper. I ignored the page in my hand. I stared after him, repeating his evaluation to myself: *beautiful*.

Was I beautiful? The question merited investigation. In study hall, I spent hours hunched over my textbooks with a compact mirror in hand, ignoring the words before me to examine my face from every angle. Between classes, I visited my reflection as often as I could, as if in danger of forgetting what I looked like. What I saw in the mirror always came as a shock to me—the unblemished skin, the fresh flush of the lips, the somewhat feline features—so that I stood there, intoxicated, for minutes on end.

I was constantly comparing myself to the girls around me and was proud to count myself among the top tier: admirably slim, clear-skinned, with nice hair and no unfortunate facial features. While I didn't exude sexual experience in the way that Siobhan Pierce or Hannah Williams or even Amanda did (from the very first, I sensed that she was not a virgin—an intuition she confirmed for me on a bus trip to San Rafael), I had a freshness that was far more rare and delicate. In purely physical terms, I wouldn't have looked too out of place standing next to the prettiest girls in my grade. The white blouses and reddish tartan of our uniforms became me. Never in my life had I felt so genetically blessed.

As one of the blessed, I rejoiced in the defects of others. There were the fat ones, who came in all different heights and colors, and who orbited the school like so many tartan-skirted planets, high socks slicing into the flesh of their calves. Perhaps even more delightfully grotesque, however, were those girls whose irregular features, irksome facial expressions, and general awkwardness combined to make me hate them on sight. There was a junior with large, purplish lips, frizzy hair, and a freakishly long neck who I often saw carrying a violin case on my way to history from my locker. Another had inky eyes, set in a broad, flat face scarred so badly by acne that, from afar, she resembled a burns victim, but also a lion (I think it was her sandy bob cut). Then there was Mitzi Gantz, a girl in my grade whose Eurasian blood, rather than producing a fine-boned, exotic beauty, had created an anomaly: slanty eyes, freckles, and an Amazonian physique, with large bones and no breasts to speak of. Had she carried herself well, she might have been perfectly acceptable; as it was, she slouched and lurked. Her messy, black hair was constantly hanging in her eyes, and she never spoke, unless forced to—at which, a husky, barely intelligible murmur would issue from her chapped lips. "Ugh, that freak," Amanda was given to saying, whenever we saw Mitzi lurching past. One weekend, we spied her in the company of a white-haired man in a yellow golf shirt and a much younger oriental woman. We could only conclude that these were her parents.

There was also a freshman girl, Karen Harmsworth's little sister. Like Mitzi, she wasn't entirely ugly. Nonetheless, my aversion to her amounted almost to a passion. Even among the freshmen, she was small. She had a beaky nose and the eyes of a husky dog. Her freckles and pale eyebrows were those of a natural strawberry blonde (Karen's color), but the hair on her head was solid black and worn in a pixie cut. The shortness of her hair meant her vulnerable nape was constantly exposed, as were her ears. These ears always seemed too red and oddly shaped, as if an animal had been gnawing on them. I once found myself behind those ears and that nape in a toilet queue, and experienced an involuntary shiver of dislike.

It was a relief to come back to my own beauty, after all this. My beauty was youthful and delicate, and didn't need to be laden with costume jewelry, of the kind that Amanda favored. In fact, my only adornment was a pair of peridot studs, which I had worn ever since my mother took me to have my ears pierced as a sniveling six-year-old. As soon as I was old enough, my mother had also taken me cosmetics shopping, telling me that I was what Mary Spillane would call "an Autumn type with hazel eyes." I still owned the selection of lipsticks that she'd chosen for me, in warm colors with boring names—cinnamon, burnt sienna, terracotta. I didn't wear them as they were, but typically blotted my lips after applying them, leaving only a trace of the original color, and escaping the attention of even Mrs. Faherty—one of those deputy types who spoke at assemblies and whose sole responsibility seemed to be upbraiding girls on their dress and comportment.

I was hopeless when it came to arranging my hair, never able to master the intricate braids and twists I saw other girls wearing. Nothing was more charming, however, than the loose, Pre-Raphaelite curls that fell to the middle of my back and needed no arranging. Having seen the way that Steadman looked at me, that day under the willows as Marcelle toyed with my hair, I knew that these curls were among my greatest assets.

IN THE last week of every month, we were given the choice to take a day trip to San Rafael. These trips began at ten A.M. sharp, when we were expected to have congregated in the main parking lot before a convoy of school buses rolled up. What was meant to be only a thirty-minute bus ride, out of sheer disorganization, always ended up taking longer. In my year at Saint Cecilia's, I only ever took advantage of three of those day trips. The first of these was in September, my first month at the school.

We sat toward the back of the bus: Amanda and Marcelle together; me in the seat behind next to Karen Harmsworth, who spent the whole journey leaning across the aisle and talking to the Smith twins. Homecoming was a week away and the girls still needed to put the final touches on their outfits. As for me, having submitted to their offer to find me a date—the seriousness of which I didn't realize until it was too late for me to back out—I had yet to find a dress.

Who my date would be was still a subject of discussion. Leaning over the back of their seat, Amanda and Marcelle chattered away about my options. "The only guy left on the rowing team is Scott Maccoby, and he's, well . . . a bit of a sleaze."

Marcelle snorted with laughter: "*You* would know!"

"Marcelle, shh. It was only that one time and . . . I told you, Marcy, shut it . . . It was nothing, really. Okay." Amanda rolled her eyes and lowered her voice. "It was a hand-job. But that's it, I swear. It's not like I *slept* with him."

I lowered my eyes and nodded primly, waiting for her to go on.

"He's not really my type, but you might like him. And he's friends with Seamus."

"And Flynn."

"And Flynn. So if you go with him, we can all sit together. You can always ditch him when we're there if you think he's too much of a sleaze."

All this sounded pragmatic enough, if distasteful. I nodded again. "Fine."

"But I want her to go with Larry!" Marcelle protested. "Laurel and Lawrence would be so cute!"

"*Laurel and Lawrence.* Oh my God, that is cute." Amanda deliberated. "But he's not friends with the rowing guys, and they'll all be at the same table. If only we'd asked earlier, we could have set her up with Xavier. Now he's taking *Therese . . .*"

By the time we arrived in San Rafael, my pairing with the illustrious Scott Maccoby seemed to have been decided. We alighted from the bus and, after a quarter hour of being instructed on how to comport ourselves, were released until five o'clock—at which point, we were to meet back in front of city hall. How we would pass six hours in that place was beyond me and, by midday, I was already sick to death of the rows of colorful, cheaply made dresses that Marcelle and Amanda suggested to me. When, after another hour of fiddling with shoulder straps and inhaling the close, conditioned air of fitting rooms, Marcelle began to whine outside my curtains about hunger pangs, I decided to abandon the project altogether. My funeral dress would suffice; there was no need to go to further lengths for Trinity boys. I exited the fitting room, coolly handing my rejections over to the pencil-browed salesgirl, who gave me a withering simper. "Nothing to your liking?" As I left the store, flanked by noisy blondes, her eyes burned into my back.

"Pizza?" Amanda queried Marcelle, when we emerged into the sunlight and exhaust.

"Pizza!" Marcelle confirmed. My opinion didn't matter; they seldom saw me eating.

All through the afternoon, Marcelle was belching, her breath revolting with the smell of second-hand garlic and pepperoni. I had put away two diet colas, ice included, and a half-pitcher of water while watching them consume their lunches—a slow, unsavory spectacle of threaded cheese, swapped slices, finger-licking, and sex-talk—and, as a consequence, was constantly needing the bathroom. On my third or fourth excursion, Amanda let out a massive groan of impatience. I paid no heed; I was lightheaded from too much walking and not enough to eat. Returning from the white fluorescence of the ladies' room, I was momentarily disoriented by the dimness inside the arcade. It took me several blinks to see that my friends had deserted me.

I sighed. Though my pride was wounded, the wound was dulled by my fundamental indifference to the matter. There was a bookstore across the way where I could pass what remained of the afternoon.

AT FIVE P.M., laden with shopping bags, Marcelle and Amanda blustered up to the steps of city hall, where I sat with my nose in a book. "Laurel! Where were you? We were looking all over!"

"We had to keep shopping without you. We didn't know *where* you went."

"Ditching us! So rude. Look, Mandy got new shoes that make her look like a dominatrix. What did you buy. . . ?"

Alas, it wasn't fine literature that I was reading, but something far cruder: a three-hundred-page volume called *The Conclusive Book of Body Language*. On the cover were two smiling chumps—psychologists who were also married—in exaggerated poses: he with his arms crossed, she with her hands on her hips. In bright red lettering, they advertised: "Get What You Want Through Non-verbal Communication." Amanda cooed when she saw it. "Oh, I *love* psychology books!"

I was still reading it on the bus ride home, in bed that evening, and over the spillages of lunch hour the following week. By far the most frequented section was one titled "Seven Signs that She has Sex on her Mind," which Marcelle and Amanda read aloud over my shoulder on Monday afternoon.

"'Number one: preening the hair. Preening in front of a man is a way for the woman to show that she cares how he perceives her. By flicking her hair back, the woman also disperses pheromones, which we all know are nature's most effective perfume.' How do I smell, Mandy?" Marcelle flicked her hair and thrust her neck in Amanda's face.

"Like B.O. Go away."

"'Number two: licking and pouting the lips. By licking and pouting her lips, the woman makes them appear fuller and wetter, signaling the ready state of her genitals . . .' Oh, yuck! Listen: 'Lipstick in bright red shades is an easy way for the woman to suggest her own flushed, engorged labia . . .'"

"Marcelle, oh, *Marcelle!*" Amanda snaked her tongue over her lips salaciously.

"'Number three: the limp wrist. Drawing attention to her weak, slender wrists allows the woman to arouse feelings of dominance and protectiveness in nearby males . . .'"

"Well, that's just stupid. You look like a queer."

"'Number four: crossing and recrossing the legs. The woman who crosses and recrosses her legs in front of a man does so to draw his attention to that part of her body . . .' blah blah blah. 'Number five: swaying the hips . . .'"

"Boring. Next."

"'Number six: self-touching.' This is a good one! 'When in the company of a man she likes, the woman may call attention to the most sensitive areas of her body, such as her neck, her thighs, and her earlobes . . .'"

"They forgot the clit."

"Mandy! '. . . Touching these areas lets her show him what he's missing out on, while also acting as a socially acceptable form of self-gratification. Number seven: touching a phallical object . . .'"

By this point, Marcelle was so crippled by laughter that she was unable to go on.

I took to consulting that list mentally during his classes, asking myself whether I was doing everything I could to capture his attention. Could he see my wrists? Were my lips wet and plump? Was I touching the sensitive skin of my body or, better still, a phallical object? I had, often enough, caught myself performing these gestures, along with other positive signals—steady eye contact, arched back, body angled toward his—without thinking. Once brought to my awareness, however, I had them down to a science, even adding flourishes of my own.

I occasionally committed the *faux pas* of wearing a black brassiere beneath my white blouse or of fiddling with my collar and buttons, in a manner reminiscent of undressing. One day, when he came and did his crouching trick by my desk, I made a point of tossing my hair from my throat, tugging at my collar and rubbing the nape of my neck, my clavicle and, beneath my shirt, my shoulder blades, as he spoke to me in smooth, murmured tones. Another time, when I noticed that he was calling girls up to his desk to discuss their essay results in private, I covertly undid an extra button of my blouse so that he could see my bra when I bent over. I'll never forget the juxtaposition between his large, hairy hand and my elongated white one over my A-grade assignment; the way that his dark eyes skimmed over my small bust as lightly as they did my face; the way he told me that my paper was meticulous and well-researched, though could have benefited from some more specific examples. "Have you read any Milton?" he asked me irrelevantly before I went back to my desk.

It was evident that he saw me, from the way that his eyes were occasionally drawn to my swinging legs or paused often and for a longer time on my face; even that he saw me as a nice-looking girl. His gaze did not betray anything further, however; no inappropriate feelings, no bubbling, uncontrollable lust. It wasn't the gaze of a felon, on the brink of committing statutory rape. At most, it was an aesthetician's glance, with just the hint of something fatherly that was also an extension of his profession—a desire to protect, perhaps, to edify and see succeed one of his most gifted and sensitive students. It was a glance that I thought I'd seen before.

ON WEDNESDAYS, we continued to see the rowers from the classroom window. I wasn't at all interested in them, but it amused me to gauge Steadman's reaction to the weekly disruption. Every Wednesday, there were jokes about forgotten binoculars and pleas for him to let us take the lesson outdoors. Mr. Steadman would fold his arms and affect weariness, before resorting to terse humor, even threats.

"Careful, girls, or I might have to have a talk with the rowing instructor about their training hours."

Or: "Marcelle, if you don't stop gawking soon, I'm going to have to draw the curtains. And that will make the room dark. And stuffy. And no fun for anyone."

He said this with a sly, gruff, tiger-glance my way—challenging me, perhaps, to find a better specimen than himself among that group of boys. If that was his game, I played along, smiling past Marcelle's shoulder with my chin in my hands. I gazed out only for as long as it took his own gaze to settle on me. Then my narrow eyes darted back to him and my lips tightened into a subtle yet knowing smile.

That I could come out with stuff like that despite my shyness and inexperience, was a testament to how well-versed I had become in the arts of seduction. Still, there were times when I forgot myself; times when, walking alone in the hallways,

I lost face completely at the sight of him. I would purse my lips instead of licking and pouting them. Instead of swinging my hips, I would tug at my kilt and attempt to pass him by as quickly as possible. I could never be sure whether I turned his head or not, at such moments. Nevertheless, I had faith in the lure of my long legs, the grace of my gracelessness.

I was convinced that I was on the right track; that I had done nothing so far to repel him. All the same, I knew that more needed to be done to set myself apart from the crowd and make a lasting impression. I considered and discarded a number of ideas, before hitting upon a plan of genius. Remembering how I had arrived late to his first lesson, and how he had stared at me so openly when I walked through the door, I was inspired to restage the scene. I wouldn't have to miss too much of his class, I assured myself: only enough to ensure that I entered the room alone and that he would be compelled to look my way.

The first time that I tried this, it was a great success. I had loitered in the restroom for some minutes after second bell, making myself pretty, before setting off at a leisurely pace for English class. As predicted, everyone turned the heads when I entered the room, including Mr. Steadman. I met his eye and read his relief, barely restrained and bordering on jubilation.

I repeated the act the next day, and the day following that. By the third time, I could see that he was suspicious; that he had come to expect the performance, without knowing exactly what it was about. Even Marcelle and Amanda had noticed that something was up, wanting to know why I was late for English and nothing else. He said nothing about his suspicions, however; only raised his dark brows and smirked, as if daring me to come later the next day. Lesson after lesson, I did just that.

It was only after it had been going on for more than a week and his smug looks had prompted me to arrive a full fifteen minutes late, that I knew the game was up. He didn't turn his head when I entered the room; merely carried on intoning, moving his hands emphatically, before assigning some pages of reading to the class. I had barely begun on the first paragraph when he called me to the desk, under the surveillance of eleven open textbooks, eleven lowered heads.

Mr. Steadman was sitting back in his chair, hands clasped behind his head and legs in the figure-four position that *The Conclusive Book of Body Language* had taught me was a crotch-display. His dark eyes were twinkling. Though he didn't smile, he seemed on the verge of doing so. I was looking down at my oxfords, one arm slung across my body to clutch the other, when he spoke.

"You are obviously very intelligent, but that doesn't mean you can get away with missing out on class time. It isn't fair to the other students. Or to me."

He was smiling by then. The whole thing was a joke to him, as it was to me. Why didn't he extend the joke, give me a detention? It was within his rights; nay, it was his duty! Instead, he merely extended his hand, reached for my wrist unexpectedly. He circled its frailty with ease between his thumb and forefinger, while drawing up the sleeve of my gray knit with his three remaining digits. Without explanation, he turned my knobby wrist around in his fingers, exposing its pale underbelly. We both stared down for a moment. Another moment . . . my heart suspended in time.

"You should wear a watch," he said.

And at that, he let me go.

I HAD been dreading the dance at Trinity since our day trip to San Rafael. Soon enough, it was upon us. Leaving him on the lawn that Friday afternoon, I couldn't have been farther from where I wanted to be.

The next day was a flurry of preparations for everyone but me. I hadn't made an appointment at the salon, as my friends had. Instead, I spent the afternoon in my arbor, reading *Paradise Lost* and deluding myself that I felt nothing of the October chill, creeping over my bare limbs. An hour before the dance, I put on my flapperish funeral dress, a light layer of cosmetics, and some black high heels. These raised me two whole inches above my usual five foot eight. I arrived at Amanda's dorm room with thirty minutes to spare. Her face fell when she saw me. "Laurel! But, Laurel, you're hardly dressed!"

She ushered me into her bedroom in a confusion of perfume and costume jewelry. Her face was made and her hair high, but she was only wearing a skimpy robe. I could see the flesh-colored bra cupping her breasts, which were the size and shape of ripe mangoes. "Where's Marcelle?" I asked, for something to say.

"Marcy? Who knows. Probably still doing her makeup. Quick, sit down. Let's see what I can do with you."

I averted my eyes as she leaned over me, breasts joggling, piling further creams and powders onto my modest efforts and making conversation like a hairdresser. Within a quarter of an hour, my face had a snide, provocative look and my hair was as high as her own. She held alternate pairs of earrings up to my face and asked, "Which ones?" I plumped for the plainer.

In a few minutes, Marcelle was scrabbling outside the door like a stray cat. "*Merde.* Laurel, can you let Marcy in?" Amanda said, shedding her robe and reaching, fully fleshed, for the orangey-red, gold-brocaded gown that hung outside her wardrobe.

"Laurel! You look like a model!" Marcelle herself was wearing turquoise. With all her cosmetics, she looked as disarmingly overdone as a child beauty queen.

"Marcy! So. Hot." Amanda smooched her lips from across the room. She was still struggling with her dress. "*Merde*, I forgot how hard this is to do up. Oh, double *merde*, these shoes are already pinching. . . !"

THE TRINITY boys proved, predictably, to be an abhorrent bunch. Seamus Head, who took Amanda's arm walking into the ballroom, was a tall, well-fleshed Alpha male with militantly cropped hair—her obvious mate, and as unappealing to me as a mountain gorilla. Flynn Radley, Marcelle's date, was arguably even worse, with the shaggy red hair and low nasal bridge of a Neanderthal, and eyes somewhere to the side of his head. I could only imagine what odd-looking children they would have had. I was still marveling over the poor taste of my friends when my own prince showed up at my elbow, leering at me with moist, hazel eyes.

"You must be Laurel Marks."

His was a Southern Californian drawl. He had too many muscles and was at least two inches shorter than I would've been without my high heels. He had a boy's haircut and swollen cheeks; his upper lip, however, was faintly but darkly mustachioed. I wondered if he had grown the thing for the occasion.

"Well, I lucked out. They told me you were pretty. Shall we?" He offered me his arm. "I'm Scott, by the way."

Each table sat four couples. Inside, we were joined by Xavier Bernard—heavy-jawed, barrel-chested, broken-nosed—and dark Therese Arras, who was quite pretty with her sleek ponytail and dash of Cherokee blood. I knew her from my math class, though had never associated with her much. We exchanged a few polite words about one another's dresses and Mr. Slawinski's teaching methods. Within minutes, our conversation had died down. Scott stroked my bare arm with a stubby index finger. "Tell me about yourself, Laurel."

I looked up, alarmed. "There's nothing to tell."

"Sure there is. You're new, aren't you? Me, I'm from San Diego. Have you been to San Diego?"

"No."

"You're missing out. But I'll be going to Stanford, so it's good for me, living up here. Do you have your top colleges picked out yet?"

He had hit upon a safe subject. "Well, I was thinking one of the Claremont colleges . . . But lately, I've been looking into Pennsylvania."

No one was to know that this was Steadman's influence; that the idea of being in the state where he had grown up thrilled me.

"Pennsylvania, huh? That's pretty far, for a girl who hasn't even been to San Diego." He nudged me in a way that was meant to be playful. "Where in Pennsylvania?"

"Swarthmore, Bryn Mawr, maybe Gettysburg . . ."

"Liberal arts all the way, then." He gave me another lingering, moist look. "You're an arty girl. A dreamy, arty girl."

After forty minutes at the table (Scott attempting to impress me with his 3.6 grade point average and the breadth of his reading—a schoolboy's Steinbeck, Hemingway, and Atticus Finch), we made the obligatory trip to the ladies' room. We weren't the only ones with this idea: there was a queue stretching far into the hallway. Eventually, we edged our way into a washroom as loud and colorful as a cage full of parakeets. "Oh my God, how weird is it seeing Flynn in a suit?"

"He looks cute!"

"That hair! Did he even brush it?" Amanda dabbed at her lips in the fraction of mirror that was visible above the other girls' heads. "Could you tell that Seamus had his hair cut?"

"Guys always look weird after having their hair cut."

"I know! But I *love* that military look on him. How's Scott?" Amanda turned to me with a glint in her eye.

I shrugged.

"Do you think he's cute?"

"He's a bit short," I said carefully.

"Sorry, I forgot to mention that. But otherwise? Do you think his face is cute? I saw you guys talking. You know, if he's boring you, we can try to find Lawrence. I think he's here with Dana, but everyone knows that was just a last-minute thing . . ."

"It's okay."

"Better to stick with our guys, anyway. They're getting us drinks right now." Amanda gave us a sly, sidelong look and—in case that wasn't enough—added in a knowing whisper, "*Actual* drinks."

There was a cup of fruit punch before me when I returned to my place at the table. I took a sip and tasted something sickly, rum or bourbon. Scott eyed me moistly over the top of his own glass.

WHILE THE spiked punch made time pass more quickly, it also made Scott Maccoby more presumptuous. I was sorry the moment I let him drag me out to the dance floor, where he wouldn't stop trying to catch hold of me and press himself upon me. "Relax," he murmured, his breath warm and disgusting against my neck. "Don't be so stiff." I had never liked dancing and Scott's attentions made it nearly impossible for me to move naturally. When he grabbed my bare arm with his stubby fingers and attempted to draw me against his chest, that was all I could take. I shook my head and yanked my arm away, giving him my sharpest glare, before swiveling back to the table.

Therese was there with Rebecca Hammel and Flora de la Roche, who glanced at me kindly as I settled back down and took a solemn sip of my punch. "You don't like your date?" Therese inquired.

"No," I replied. "I like somebody else."

I regretted my words straight away. Suddenly, I wanted Steadman with a force that practically winded me. I yearned to say his name aloud, to condemn him for making it so hard for me to breathe. It was agony to think that he was alive at that very moment, healthy and content with his wife and children, not sparing a thought for me. As long as I was tortured by love for him, I wanted him to be just as miserable as I was.

AFTER THE social overtime of San Rafael and Homecoming, I felt that I'd earned myself the right to be withdrawn, at least for a few weeks. I began giving Marcelle and Amanda the slip in favor of what I called "college applications"—really just protracted sessions of daydreaming about Steadman while flicking through pamphlets. Hiding out in the lofted section of the library, I stared into space, scratching out sentences between one sigh and the next.

As well as being the subject of my daydreams, Steadman had begun to inhabit my dreams at night. These dreams were never sexually explicit. Most often, they involved him smiling and making obscure, faintly embarrassing requests in a dream-jargon whose exact terminology I forgot within minutes of waking. The symbolic content of these dreams was easy enough for me to interpret as he sat in his chair holding out a thick pen or caressing the rim of his coffee mug.

Less common and more difficult for me to bear were the dreams in which we kneeled together, post-coitally. I would see nothing of the act that had just occurred or of our naked bodies—only a dim room filled with book crates and his beaming face. He would stroke my hair and in the warmest, most paternal manner possible, tell me that everything was okay, that we were in love, and that our love had already been consummated. I would ask him how this had come about, telling him that I remembered nothing, that it was all like a dream to me. At that, everything would dissolve into a heap of tender, hushing caresses. Awake, I'd lay in the dark for some moments, asking myself the same questions, trying to remember when the act of consummation had occurred, until the ceiling seemed to crumble down on me—leaving me with a taste of bitter dust, black heartache, and a keen desire for death.

It had gotten to the stage where my choice seemed to be between consummation and death. Since consummation was death, however, I didn't have a choice at all. One way or another, I was soon to die, and this knowledge made me careless of myself, apparently immune to pain. I bruised my body without knowing how I did so, ate less than ever. I suffered a bad head cold one week in October but attended his class anyway, only to be sent to the sick bay by Ms. Da Silva the lesson after. I was prescribed lots of fluids and the rest of the week in bed, a fate that I accepted with relief, once I got over the initial despair of not being able to see him. My friends, who came to visit me on the Thursday afternoon, told me that my love had been asking after me; that it had upset him to hear that I was unwell. Suddenly, I was reminded of what a gentleman he was, of how courtly his behavior had always been toward me. I had visions of deathbed romances, of dying mysterious and pure like Dante's Beatrice, and yearned to be afflicted with something more serious than a common cold.

I had them collect my homework from him. The next afternoon, they handed me a note in his barely legible red ink.

Laurel—

    Read the chapter on Byron (but only if you are up to it!).

    Have a look at some of the shorter poems—She walks in Beauty, To a Beautiful Quaker, etc. (but again, only if you are up to it, and only if it pleases you). I will compile some annotations to give to you on ~~Mo~~ Tuesday.

    Most importantly, do not strain yourself. Get plenty of rest. Recuperate. I will be glad to bring you up to date with everything next lesson.

                 Warmest regards,

                 Hugh

Hugh! I couldn't help it—my eyes misted up a little upon seeing that. The others were talking about their plans with Seamus and Flynn, what a shame it was that we couldn't make it a triple date. When they had gone, I thrust my face into the pillow, sighing with pent-up desire. By the end of the weekend, the scrap of paper had become softened, the ink running in places, from all the times that I'd pressed the note to my lips. Likewise, the portrait of Lord Byron in my textbook was on the receiving end of many congested kisses, as it occurred to me how much the poet resembled my beloved.

As LUCK would have it, Marcelle caught my cold and was absent on Tuesday morning, my first day back in his classroom. This allowed him to attend to me more openly than he might otherwise have done, crouching by my desk and going through various interpretations of the poems they'd discussed the week before. "And your friend, where is she?" he asked me, some five minutes into the catch-up session, as if only just noticing Marcelle's absence. Unfortunately, it could not go on forever. The class was in anarchy without his direction. "I'd better take care of that," he murmured in my ear, unexpectedly hot, close, and conspiratorial, when one of the girls shrieked on the other side of the room. I turned to regard the seat of his corduroys—one hand cupped to my ear, in an effort to contain the condensation left by his words—only to have my glance intercepted by Amanda. I blanched. How much had she seen, exactly?

Later in the week, he found some other pretext to crouch by my desk for an extended period, thumbing through my textbook and stopping at a stanza that I had underlined. He read this stanza aloud in his resonant voice.

Weep, daughter of a royal line
A sire's disgrace, a realm's decay;
Ah! happy if each tear of thine
Could wash a father's fault away!

"You like these lines? Why?" he wanted to know. "What do they mean to you?"

I blushed and spouted off something embarrassing, I barely remember what, about a royal line polluted by the vices of the father, inherited decay, original sin. He gave me a peculiar look and told me that this was an interesting interpretation of what was essentially a rather obscure, forgettable political poem. Mortified, I cast my eyes away. For the rest of the conversation, I crossed my arms and met his carefully placed questions with one-word answers.

As he went on to cater to others and I to hunch over my books, I felt his gaze returning to me from across the room. Looking up, I saw that his expression was fixed, sober. I didn't doubt that I was in his thoughts, yet the obscurity of these thoughts filled me with dread. It was the first time since meeting him that I felt the true peril of what I had gotten myself into. He had seen me. He would know me, soon enough.

It was beginning to seem like I could do nothing right, like the strings that had previously connected my mind to my body had somehow been severed. Every day, I distanced myself further from my friends. I was no longer a novelty to them and sensed private jokes forming in my absence. Suspicions flitted in their clear, cold eyes.

In the lunchroom, I was the token anorexic, anxiously nibbling on a Red Delicious while everyone else tucked into their hot meals. They would talk in their usual vulgar way——Amanda going into detail about Seamus' body; Marcelle cackling and making silly comments—while I sat in torment, gnawed by hunger and love. In my torment, it was difficult for me to keep the pain from showing on my face, to keep my fists from clenching, and to control the awful lump rising in my throat. When it got this bad, I had to get out of there, rising unannounced and ignoring their confused inquiries. By the third or fourth time I did this, they no longer called after me, instead whispering something among themselves and erupting into giggles. I found out later that a quip had developed around my sudden, unexplained departures and that they now said it every time. "Oh, look, she's gone to throw up her apple."

I did go to the bathroom, but not to throw up, nor to self-harm, self-pleasure, or even cry. The impulse to do all these things was there, but not the resolve, as I sat with my feet up inside the locked cubicle, locked in a paroxysm of self-hatred, desire, and despair. I would stay locked in place until the bell went for final period, or something else—a flush from a neighboring cubicle, or a gaggle of sophomores outside, snapping gum and spraying aerosols—came along to break the spell. Pushing past them, through their headache-inducing scents, I would run cool water and regard my dark-eyed reflection, whose savage, love-starved look always came as a shock to me.

Although no good could come of it, I sometimes chose to wander the lonely halls of the English department, shuffling numbly between the teachers' lounge and my locker, rather than hiding out in the library or returning to the lunchroom. I didn't know whether I truly desired to see Steadman, or if I haunted his department merely out of force of habit; nevertheless, I could only go undetected for so long. It would only be a matter of time before he caught a glimpse of my fleeting figure in the bright slice of a door left slightly ajar, or distinguished my soft, dragging footfalls in the hallway.

I expected him to ambush me. What I didn't expect was the direction from which he would do so, presuming that he spent all of his lunch hours in the staffroom with the other teachers. In fact, he'd been lying in wait in a lair of his own, listening as I passed from the staffroom to my locker, lingered, sighed, and turned back in the direction whence I had come. He timed his exit from the classroom to coincide exactly with the moment that I reached the door, greeting me effusively, "Hello Laurel!" he beamed. "Isn't this a pleasant surprise!"

"I'm just . . . coming from my locker."

"Well!" he was still beaming, his face flushed and eyes glinting, as if drunk. He was standing quite close and I couldn't help hoping, fearing, that he was about to bend down and kiss me, right there in the hall where anyone could see us. He laughed, probably at my expense. "Don't let me keep you!"

I stood staring, processing his words, until he laughed again. God, I loved his laugh; I loved his features, crinkling with laughter. We stared at one another for a while longer, until his smile softened, faded. I glimpsed something restless in his eyes, a glimmer of desire that I wasn't meant to see, as his glance skipped from me to his empty classroom and back to me again. Noticing this, I bowed my head and plucked my skirt in a sort of frantic curtsy. I could feel his eyes following me down the hall after I had turned my back on him, but didn't have the heart to enjoy it: I was too unnerved, too confronted by what I had seen.

IT WAS clear that we had taken it to a point beyond mere flirtation. It was no longer necessary for us to interact, to play games the way we'd been doing for weeks on end. Instead, we watched one another: he, with a proprietary coolness that suggested he already had possession of me; I, from the corners of my eyes—intent on gaining some control over his chameleonic character.

Cynical, self-deprecating, affected, indiscriminate, patronizing, immature, as sloppy intellectually as he was with his desk, fickle, vain, virile, brooding, pedantic, philandering . . . in short, Byronic, Byronic, Byronic, almost to the point of parody. It was only fitting that we should be learning about the Byronic male from a living, breathing specimen who was as much aware of his dark charms as I was. It didn't matter how many negative attributes I ascribed to his name—each one only added more flesh to the archetype, made him more whole and tangibly mine.

I was the only one in the class who understood the more cynical of his jokes, who picked up on his more recondite references, who appreciated his genius. I was the only one who saw the lonely figure he cut standing at the window like a deflated version of the *Wanderer Above the Mist*, tacked on the wall behind him. I was the only one who pitied him, seeing how the other girls occasionally reared away from his excessive spirits, the manic edge to his cheerfulness. I was the only one who adored him in the blueness of his sulks and the blackness of his tempers; the only one who stood in awe of him at his golden best, skimming stones and quoting Dante in the original Italian. I was the only one in the world who wanted him; the only one who was made for him; the only one who craved the unbuckling of his belt, the flicker of his poet's tongue. I was the only one who saw him as a man and loved him as a god.

I could feel myself crumbling, growing ever more masochistic, as the desire to taste our love, the cleaved fruit and flesh and blood of it, overwhelmed my imagination. In private, I broke my rule of not putting my feelings on paper, drafting love letters that God only knows whether I actually intended on sending to him. Though they were all torn up in the end, they were more or less reworkings of the same arguments, expressed with the same sticky metaphors, in the same madwoman's rhetoric.

Dear Sir,

I know that it is wrong, that it is against all the dictates of reason, propriety, and morality to be writing to you in this manner, but all I can say is that I do not care. You have made me unreasonable, improper, immoral. Every day that I spend in your presence, I become a little more indecent, a little more lowly and self-deprecating. It is time that I bare all, that I make myself explicit—if indeed I still have a self. I am so afflicted, sir, that I have no other option but to confess that I want you.

I want you. There was a time when I may have been able to express the sentiment less crudely, yet it is too late now.

I no longer understand how to quiver modestly, how to hide sweet, delicate blushes. Now I am wracked with convulsions, burned by the fires of hell. If I am a virgin, it is only in the most trivial, membranous sense of the word. Please, make my damnation official. I ask only that you rid me of this technicality.

I am aware that you are a professional man, a married man, a father. You may also be a religious man, and feel that what I am asking of you is an unspeakable sin. I hope that you will remember, however, that beneath all this, you are still a man. It is the man in you that I wish to appeal to, as it is the man in you that appeals to me. Were you not such a man, you would not have had this effect on me. I was pure once; I once believed in the dictates of reason, God. Now I see no reason, I believe in no god, unless you be counted. Let me stroke your ego. Let me make you my god. I beg you.

I do not ask for you to love me. In fact, were you to declare your love for me at this moment, I would spit on it, I would laugh in your face. Your love cannot save me. The best thing you could do for me would be to relieve me of myself, to take me and use me as you see fit. I do not care how you do it, or where: a bed of coals, a motel room, or (if you will permit me to be sentimental) beneath the very evergreens where you first wiped these tears and sparked these flames.

Bear in mind that I am young, nubile, and reasonably pretty. If all this does not please you, bear in mind simply that I am female, and that I am offering myself to you as a slave, who will do all the things that a wife would never dream of. I may be young, but I understand what I am proposing. You must understand, sir, that I am prepared for absolutely everything.

I promise that I can be discreet. You have said yourself that I am intelligent, and must know by now that I am by nature secretive and not liable to speak a word of what goes on between us. You are my master, my confessor. What is more, you are my teacher, and there is still so much I have to learn.

Your Eager Pupil

I had laid my mind out on the page for him and couldn't see how he could fail to be convinced by it. In fact, had this letter made it into his hands, I don't know how he would have received it. It is very possible that the audacity of the letter, and the violence of the emotions expressed might have deterred him. After all, he was a dominant male, swollen with stupid male pride, and may not have appreciated having his conquest undermined by the ravings of the very sex-starved schoolgirl he aimed to conquer. I could imagine him dismissing the letter as inappropriate in a fit of conventionality or sham guilt, and going on to refer me to the school counselor; to request my transfer to a different class; to betray me by playing the part of calm, responsible adult—hypocrite of hypocrites.

I HAD little more than a week left of life as I knew it. Under-rested, undernourished, yet essentially intact, my life as I knew it was ebbing. I had been up past lights out working on a masterpiece of a letter, which had since been folded and sealed into the thin white hope of an envelope, stamped with the S.C.C.S. crest. Even after slipping it into my satchel for the day, I still didn't know whether I actually intended on giving it to him—and, if so, how I would achieve the task. Handing it to him face-to-face would be too embarrassing; leaving it behind for him to discover, on my desk or among his papers, could too easily go wrong—lost, overlooked, fallen into the wrong hands, or sucked up by some cleaner's soulless vacuum. The best way, I thought, would be to catch his eye and drop it pointedly as I passed him or to visit him at his desk and—after much fidgeting and sweet, irrelevant questioning about the upcoming essay—place it before him before moving along, no explanations given. By the time that his class came around, however, last period of the day, I still hadn't decided on a plan of attack and was beginning to question the validity of my "masterpiece."

Worse than that, the man whose eye I hoped to catch was making the task almost impossible for me. He hardly gave me a second glance when I entered the room, and couldn't be drawn by any of the showy gestures or looks I shot his way. In fact, he wasn't at all himself that afternoon, but in a state of distraction, drumming his fingers on the tabletop and looking out of the window every few minutes. Halfway through the lesson, having instructed us to revise for Tuesday's in-class essay, he got up from his chair and left the room altogether.

I watched the clock anxiously. All around me, the murmurs of conversation were rising, reveling in his absence, as I counted ten minutes, fifteen minutes, of him being gone. It was clear to me then that he did not care for me at all; that he had never viewed his classes with me as anything other than work, time to be wiled. I felt ashamed, and worse, dead depressed, at the thought of the letter in my bag—less a masterpiece than a total embarrassment. No, he didn't care at all: not for my face, nor my legs, nor my mind, nor, least of all, for my feelings. I had no claim whatsoever on his heart.

As I was thinking this, there came a rapping on the classroom door. A woman who I'd never seen before peeked her head into the room and, flustered at finding it occupied, seemed about to slide it shut again, when she caught the sympathetic eye of Christina Tucci. Half-stepping into the room, the woman—slender, neatly dressed, aged in her mid-to-late thirties—leaned across to Christina, whispering something behind a dainty hand. The pale gold of her wedding band caught the light from the ceiling. Her silky blond hair, which was cut to her chin, flashed with the same light. Christina pointed outside and the woman smiled, shyly mouthing a thank you. She was gone as suddenly as she had come.

The trouble was, she wasn't gone. If only I'd kept my eyes from following her figure out of the door, and closed my ears to the murmurings around me, I could've prevented the fatal knowledge from dawning. There was a stirring of curiosity about the room, in which I heard the word repeated: wife, wife. It was not every day that we caught a glimpse of a teacher's spouse.

I watched through the slice of doorway, along with the rest of the class, as the lady was waylaid in the hallway by our dark-haired master. There was an upturning of palms on his part, a rueful shrug, before he glanced at his watch, nodded in the direction of the teachers' lounge, and kissed her briskly on the cheek. I noted bitterly that in her low, sling-back heels she reached as high as his cheekbone—the same height I was when I stood before him in my oxfords.

"You can go early, sir, if you have somewhere else to be," Marcelle quipped when he re-entered the room. He laughed off the comment, yet, I noticed, was unable to bring himself to look in the direction whence it had come. The last ten minutes of the lesson were taken up by his transparent attempts to make up for forty whole minutes of neglect—something that I hated him for, with every splinter of my shattered heart. As the bell went, he wished us a good weekend: ". . . though not too good. You have your essays to write on Tuesday." I could not even begin to imagine how I would survive until then.

W<small>HILE ANOTHER</small> would have fled the scene at once, to lick her wounds in private, I was intent on making the bad situation worse for myself. Having shaken off my friends at the nearest bathroom, I turned back in the direction of my locker, possessed by a dangerous desire to see more. My hands were shaking as I turned my combination; I hung my head, concealed doubly by the cold metal door and the warm curtain of my auburn curls. I stood that way for ten deep breaths as schoolgirls filtered out of the area, attempting to dull the thudding of my heart. At last, I sensed movement farther ahead, and peered over the top of my locker. Sure enough, coming from the faculty lounge was Mr. Steadman, clad in his navy sport coat and arm-in-arm with his lady. I closed the door of my locker promptly, pressing an armload of books to my chest, and started forth in their direction with my chin held high. Steadman had his head inclined toward his wife and was speaking with small, intimate gestures. My eyes flashed at him, black and bright with pride's suppressed tears. With my shield of books and my hair streaming out behind me, I was impossible to overlook. As I neared him, I saw something anxious come into his eyes—a pleading, craven look. His lips faltered on his story. This acknowledgment lasted only a fraction of a second, before his eyes glossed over and the factitious flow of his gestures was resumed. I lowered my eyes. We passed one another. She saw nothing, nothing.

In my chest, my dulled heart was hammering once again, spreading hot poison through my body. Angry tears burned at the corners of my eyes. Stopping at a trashcan, I rummaged in my bag for the envelope and shredded the whole thing to pieces, cursing his cowardice.

I<small>F</small> I didn't end things then, it was only out of spite—a desire to haunt, to hurt the one who had hurt me. I had considered, among more drastic measures, not attending his classes that week; on Tuesday morning, however, I was there to write my essay and avoid his shining coward's eyes. I avoided his eyes as he handed me my question sheet. Noticing my coolness, he was swift to move along, down-headed and in no doubt about his culpability. He didn't linger to speak with any of the other girls—something I might have been consoled by, had my spirit not been so broken. I wrote steadily, dutifully, intent on closing my mind to the awareness of his gray herringbone trousers and his gleaming belt buckle as he made his rounds. One thing was clear: I would never be free as long as I desired him.

The lesson left me more depressed than I'd begun it. My attendance had done nothing but broaden the gulf between us, into something that could not be bridged without excusing his disloyalty. How unfair it seemed to me that I should be the one to relinquish my pride, when it was *he* who had behaved badly, who had undone all our weeks of delicate maneuverings and hard-won intimacies with one indelicate action.

Though I intended to treat him haughtily, I was in fact meeker than ever. I didn't think I could look at him without tears welling up in my eyes, or speak to him without my voice betraying me, dissolving into sobs. I could scarcely look anywhere but at my own feet, shuffling between classes, and didn't dare utter a word to anyone, for fear of dislodging the lump in my throat. Over my melancholy, I wore a mask of blankness, which never fully disguised the downward quirking of the corners of my mouth.

I felt as if I'd been thinned, flattened, drained of all color. In the hallways, laughter scattered all around me, as I was elbowed, battered, pushed from place to place. November had begun, and I had taken to wearing my gray school sweater every day, a garment that made my complexion appear more white-washed than ever and the shadows beneath my eyes a deeper reddish purple. Black stockings made pins of my slim legs. I was far from the near-naked girl he'd discovered in greener days, beneath the laurel trees. Instead, I was like the dead leaf in that poem of Verlaine's, which we recited that week during French class.

> Les sanglots longs
> Des violons
> De l'automne
> Blessent mon cœur
> D'une langueur
> Monotone.
>
> Tout suffocant
> Et blême, quand
> Sonne l'heure,
> Je me souviens
> Des jours anciens
> Et je pleure
>
> Et je m'en vais
> Au vent mauvais
> Qui m'emporte
> Deçà, delà,
> Pareil à la
> Feuille morte.[1]

---

1. *The long sobs of the violins of autumn wound my heart with a monotonous languor. All choked and pale, when the hour chimes, I remember days of old and I cry. And I'm going on an ill wind that carries me here and there, as if a dead leaf.*

All choked up and pale, I was in the hall when the hour sounded for fourth period, gathering my books from the locker. It was Friday, the end of a week that had been nothing but an exercise in avoidance and self-abasement. I had been avoiding trips to the locker, avoiding routes that took me past his classroom, particularly in the onrush between one period and another. By some fateful slip of mind, however, I found myself back there to fetch my biology book, just as he was standing by the door and farewelling the last of his sophomores. He had a free period then, I knew. Framed in his doorway with his hands on his hips, he was looking away, probably pondering whether to spend the hour in the staffroom or to stay where he was. I thought that I would be safe, in my gray-sweatered plainness, to slip by him. Boldly, foolishly, he intercepted my sharp elbow, stopping me in my tracks and pronouncing my name with keen sonority. "Laurel!"

I don't know why he did it: whether it was instinct, a moment's amnesia, or whether he thought that the silence between us had simply gone on for too long, and wished to make it up to me, to force himself upon me, to smother my scruples with smiling friendliness. As I turned around to look at him, however, his hand still grasping my elbow, I knew I'd been right in keeping my eyes from his: I wasn't strong enough to sustain even a moment's contact. I looked at him in a shock of agony. As predicted, the tears had sprung.

He knew, had to know, what it was all about and that it was all his doing. I almost felt sorry for him, so quickly did his smile fade and his good intentions dissipate. I was not the woman for him: I was nothing but heartache, exasperation, needless melancholy. At the same time, I was aware that he couldn't be trusted; that the classroom behind him was empty and would be empty for some time; that he was only a matter of heartbeats, a tug of my elbow, and a few whispered words away from pulling me into that room with him. I wanted it; I couldn't bear it. I broke away.

I WALKED to the woods with my hands inside my coat pockets, fondling the canister of my father's pills as another might have fondled a revolver. In fact, I didn't have much need for the coat: it was a day of glare and white clouds, thick enough to trap whatever warmth came through. Having dumped my satchel in the dormitory, however, I had nowhere else to keep the pills. Besides, I was prepared to wait until nightfall, by which point it would no doubt be cooler.

By the time I located my laurel arbor, lunch hour was almost up. I settled between the twin trunks as I had done on count-less weekends before then, reeling from the heady scent of the leaves. In the distance, I could hear the bell for fifth period and couldn't help thinking of the sunburst-carved door of his classroom sliding open, the girls filing in from lunch, and my beloved looking as I had last seen him. The thought of going back to him glimmered in my mind. I rejected it promptly. It wouldn't be right unless he came to me.

I was asking too much of him, I knew. It was too much to expect him to decide whether I lived or not, to respond to an ultimatum he knew nothing about. Huddled beneath the laurel, I felt how slim my chances of survival really were, and sobbed at the impossibility of me making it out of those woods alive. The hour slipped by, indifferent to my suffering. From the grounds below, I heard the end-of-day bell sounding. I closed my eyes and rested my head on my knees. My heart gave a violent wrench. I counted ten minutes, twenty min-utes, without him having come. Then, soft and swift, came a rustling of leaves all around me. I looked up and saw him standing above me, overwrought in his tweeds and white shirt.

"Oh!" he cried out, a crippled sound. "Oh, my girl."

And he fell over me, covering my face with kisses, framing my face with his hands, moving his hands over my thin shoulders, under my thick coat. He removed me from my coat, letting it bunch under us, in the dirt. I tried to sit up, offering my lips for a live kiss, a waking kiss. He pulled me back down, kissing my neck instead and tugging at my sweater. My god, things were moving so fast. "Do you want this?" he muttered between kisses. "Do you want this?" My cold, blunt fingers dug into the skin of his neck. I rasped, sobbed. The death rattle of the pills in my coat pocket was the only answer that I could provide.

Part Three

I've never known a silence like that which came over us, once he had done what he had to do. The sky had darkened to a velvety blue and, against it, the laurel leaves were as black as thorns. I lay on my back, naked save for my kilt, and trying not to think too hard about the bloodshed, the dampness inside me, and everything that I'd lost. He stroked my arm, said my name. I felt raw to the touch, even there—as if a layer of my skin had been stripped away, along with the essential membrane. I began to cry.

He was very kind. He took me in his arms and made his apologies, letting me wipe my tears on his shirtfront, as on that first day. Though disheveled—his shirttails out, his trousers unbuckled—he was dressed, and I was grateful for this; I didn't think I could stand to feel his skin against mine, so soon after the fact. It wasn't long until my eyes were dry again, though my voice was mournful as I broke away to ask him, "Are we lovers now?"

"You make it sound like a death sentence," he laughed bitterly. "No, we don't have to be. Not if it hurts you. This was bliss for me, but I don't want to hurt you any more than I already have."

I began to cry again, despite myself.

"What is it now?" he asked warily.

I threw myself upon him, caressing him, kissing him amidst sobs. *Please, love me,* I wanted to say. *Please, don't leave me. Don't ever say that again.*

He must have been regretting involving himself with such a volatile young creature. Nevertheless, some masculine instinct for flattery told him what I needed, what I wanted to hear. My name was repeated, along with terms of endearment— "sweetness," "my nymph," "my glory"—and words to the effect that he loved me, that I was sacred in his eyes, and that he would never be more than a brute, a crazed fool who had stumbled upon me in the woods and defiled me. I told him that I loved him; that I was bound to him forever; that I wanted to be his lover, no matter what. I told him that he could have me again and he moaned gratefully, telling me it didn't work that way, that a man needed time in between. He kissed me on the mouth and told me that I should get dressed, that I must be freezing, turning away tactfully to zip and buckle his trousers.

I ferreted in the undergrowth for my bra and panties, dressing with my frail spine toward him. He watched me as I buttoned my blouse with trembling hands and shook my hair out over the top of my sweater. In the distance, buildings loomed, bright-windowed through the night-blackened woods. "It's late. You should be getting back to your friends," he said. "You should be getting back to your wife," I responded, with less levity than I had intended.

It was only the first time, yet already I felt that my life had become infinitely more complicated. He left me on the edge of the woods with a deep, lingering kiss and a promise that he'd find me on Monday; that we'd be together again as soon as possible. I shied away from the thought, even as I nodded and leaned in to give him my lips one more time before we parted. He turned south, in the direction of the parking lot. I headed west, past the sleeping science wing and toward the dormitories.

In the corridor of my dorm, I almost collided with Sadie Bridges, who informed me that I should hurry if I wanted to make it to dinner. I shook my head speechlessly. I had no desire to be seen in the dining hall, feeling that all the evidence of the wretched deed was written in my rumpled uniform, my unkempt tresses, and the odor that clung to me—an unpleasant odor like bleach, covering up something rank, humid, and feminine. I went to the washroom and ran myself a bath, stripping off my clothes in the misting mirror. Inspecting my naked form for changes, I thought that I could perceive a certain ripe, tarnished quality that hadn't always been there. I turned away in self-disgust.

I could only hope that what I had read about the contraceptive properties of hot bathwater were true, lowering myself into the steaming tub. I closed my eyes and lay back, welcoming the sterile tide as it washed away the sin, with its residue of blood, dirt, and seed. When I tried to recall the act, I instantly felt his weight upon me and a splitting pain between my legs. There was no pleasure to recall; all the same, I felt my lips burning at the memory, and a throbbing in my loins. I recognized this at once for what it was: the curse of renewed desire.

I may as well have spent that evening in hell, so extreme and variable were my emotions. There was despair, which had me sobbing, dry-eyed, into my pillow, and thinking desperately of the canister of pills—still in my coat pocket, and as well-stocked as it had been that afternoon. There was disgust: for myself, for my lover, and for the sordid, undignified act. There was fear, physical and spiritual. There was delirium, sweet and fey and frenzied, which could have seen me stripping off my clothes or, just as easily, tearing off my own flesh in strips.

There was repentance, which had me yearning to be a child again, in my mother's arms, hidden from the world of men. Finally, there was the desire, constant as a heartbeat, which made suicide and repentance equally impossible.

By morning, I was numb. Unable to cope with the emotional turmoil of the night before, I had forced myself to adopt a new construct of feeling: one that did not distinguish among any of the prior sentiments or even the more fleeting, positive stirrings of triumph and tenderness. It was as if I were looking out over the whole spectrum of my emotions all at once—a mountain scape of blissful peaks, crags, and lows. Naturally, this made it difficult for me to act, even think. On Saturday afternoon, I took my books to the library and was less productive than ever. At Sunday Mass, I was unmoved by the sermon and found myself staring instead at the stained-glass windows of the chapel: pure, glazed windows that reminded me of my broken state, the sanctity from which I was eternally severed.

I still hadn't managed to break out of my passivity by Monday, though I remembered Steadman's promise that he would seek me out. Instinctively, I clung to my companions, hardly daring to venture from one classroom to the next without another girl by my side, acting as my *dueña*. The two occasions when I did glimpse him from afar, walking alongside Mr. Wolfstein and standing outside his classroom with a coffee mug in hand, I felt faint and didn't allow myself to be seen. Our promises to meet each other again as soon as possible died away with last period, where I sat beside Marcelle drawing staid Japanese mountain scapes in black ink.

That evening, I found myself fretting over the broken engagement, half-convinced that it was he who had been avoiding me and that his passion must have cooled over the weekend. My former ambivalence was forgotten as I pined after Mr. Steadman, counting the hours until our inevitable meeting in the next morning's English class. I selected my undergarments with care and laid them out with my uniform, letting my imagination run wild with thoughts of how free we really were, the unlimited caresses and compliments that would now be showered upon me—provided I could keep him interested.

In the morning, I took extra pains to make myself presentable, staining my lips "cinnamon" and donning an Alice band to keep my hair off my face. I arrived at his class in a flurry after biology, my cheeks flushed from the cold. He was cleaning the blackboard with small, fussy gestures. There was a vase of red chrysanthemums on his desktop. We were not yet alone, so our eyes could only meet briefly. Nevertheless, I noticed his suppressed smile of tenderness and felt myself responding; felt my body softening as the morning light, with all its dancing dust motes, flooded through the window and into my heart.

He was fluent, he was limpid, he conducted himself with ease. He shot me meaningful glances, full of black, liquid fire, as he read from *Don Juan*—seeking my face with every mention in the poem of the words "heart," "love," and "desire." As for me, I didn't take my eyes off him, sitting back in my chair with my legs gracefully crossed and my hands folded in my lap. I sat in my newly acquired wisdom, watching him and reminding myself that the lines of his body were known to me; that the touch of his hands was known to me; that the lips he recited with had been in contact with my lips only days ago. He was mine, all mine—never mind the strip of gold on his finger, the three days we'd spent apart. I rejoiced in my knowledge of him, which made me feel as privileged as a visionary who's just seen the face of God.

He had us close our books five minutes before time was up so he could hand back our essays from the week before.

One by one, the other eleven girls were called up to collect their work—some returning to their desks with scowls, some beaming. By the time that the bell went, my name still hadn't been announced. My classmates clattered to clear the room. "How odd, Laurel, I can't seem to find your essay." He smiled at me as I approached his desk, making a show of rifling through his papers. "Give me a moment, it must be in one of these files . . ."

AFTER THE last girl had slipped through the door, Steadman smirked and retrieved my paper from where it had been lying the whole time, facedown at his elbow. As I reached in to accept it, he took hold of my wrist, swiftly pulling up the sleeve of my gray sweater. Laughing, I loosed myself and made for the door against his protests. He was silenced when he saw me slide the door shut and bolt it from the inside. I glanced at my grade and returned to him, simpering as I stashed the paper inside my satchel.

"Oh, you sly thing." He patted his knee. "Come, sit with me."

I hesitated. I had never sat on a man's knee before.

"Come on." He held me by the waist and drew me closer to him. I settled awkwardly on his lap and, immediately feeling his response, lowered my eyes.

"You're still shy of me, aren't you?" he said in a sugary voice, somewhat patronizing. "We'll have to work on that."

I shrugged and shook my head.

"I won't bite, you know." He sat back from me slightly—a teacher again, despite the bulge in his trousers.

"I don't mind if you do."

"Oh, my girl." He thumbed my cheek. "You don't know what you're saying."

Maybe I didn't. In any case, I couldn't think of anything else to say. Our first conversations were really all something of a failure. In fact, when I think about it, we were only ever able to talk freely after making love. We didn't have time to make love then.

Instead, I shuffled forward in his lap, making him sigh inadvertently. I brushed my fingers over his collar and blinked down at his tie, with its pattern of golden spears or arrowheads. I waited a long heartbeat, before giving him an amateurish, wet kiss. He accepted it graciously.

As our kisses grew deeper and longer, he must have noticed the discrepancy between my callow enthusiasm, which left his chin slick with saliva, and his refinements—refinements that struck me as somewhat grotesque at the time. I didn't know how to respond to the sucking and nibbling of my lower lip, or the tongue artfully arching and caressing my own. His breath, teachers' breath, tasted faintly of coffee. His hands smoothed over my hips and up to my small breasts, groping them through the wool of my sweater. I was becoming very hot and bothered with the knowledge that the bell would be going any minute, that the halls would be flooded any minute with girls refreshed from their morning break, and that I wouldn't be able to find relief in time. It was a relief then, in an anticlimactic way, when the bell did go and I jumped up from his lap, away from the source of my anxiety.

"This isn't the first time we've been interrupted by one of those," he said of the bell, in allusion to our first encounter. "Nor do I think it will be the last."

I mumbled something about getting to math class and he nodded, stroked my leg in acquiescence. As I reached the door, he called my name. "Laurel! When can I see you again. . . ?"

OUR FIRST true rendezvous took place on Wednesday after third period. I had gone from his class to gym, changing into my red costume and getting my name marked off the list as usual. I had even run along with the rest of the class, past the tennis courts and toward the oval, cutting through the shrubbery. As a fine, mist-like rain began to fall, I took the opportunity to duck behind the bushes, where I waited for the last of the joggers to pass. By the time I made it to the English department, having turned back to collect my things from the locker room, I was quite drenched and the hour was more than half up. I locked the door behind me as he bolted up from his chair and came to meet me in the middle of the room, where he was to have me for the second time ever.

It was carpet burn and good, plain *missionarsstellung*, just as God had intended it—my soaking gym clothes piled in a corner of the room, between the wastepaper basket and the radiator. Against my expectations, it hurt just as much as the first time: more, even, for then I had been overcome with emotion, whereas that Wednesday afternoon in the well-lit classroom, I was perfectly lucid. All the same, I didn't cry; in fact, I did what I could to accommodate him, wrapping my legs around his back and sighing into his ear to speed the whole thing up. At the vital moment, he pulled out—an unexpected wrench that pained me almost as much as the first, expected thrust—and, to my dismay, spilled his warmth all over my rain-glistening stomach.

The rain outside was coming down in heavy sheets, which crashed against the windowpanes like gunfire. At some point during his last loving labors, the lunch bell had sounded. From the halls beyond, we could hear the muffled chattering of schoolgirls who preferred to crowd together undercover rather than brave the downpour. He mumbled grateful nothings into my ear. He kissed my petal-mouth, the tips of my pale breasts. He went to his desk for tissues. "Was it better this time?" he wanted to know, dabbing at my stomach. "Yes," I lied. Such was the miserable business that I'd gotten myself into.

We spent an hour together in the claustrophobic tenderness of each other's arms and the heat of the radiator. As he stroked and fondled my young body, telling me that he'd never known such smooth skin, such lovely legs, such delicacy and tightness, I shyly inspected his own body from above. Though there was little beauty about the underarm hair, the chest hair, and the hair that grew across his belly, the sight of all this inspired me with awe, so marvelous was the contrast between his dark, hirsute virility and my insipid loveliness. Out of a desire to exaggerate this contrast, I reached for his wrist and removed his brown and gold watch, fitting it, at its tightest setting, halfway up my forearm. Predictably, he complimented my slenderness. I proceeded to try on his gold wedding band, swiveling it about the joint of my ring finger and asking him how many years he'd been married (sixteen), whether he got along well with his wife.

"Oh, yes," he effused. "Danielle is a wonderful person."

He went on to tell me tactfully that he obviously didn't love her, the mother of his children, as he loved me; that he'd never loved anyone as forcefully and inevitably as he loved me; that he hoped I didn't think badly of him for betraying her. I assured him that I didn't, adding that I wasn't bothered in the least by the fact that he was married.

As strange as it may seem, I really had the utmost respect for the sacred covenant of marriage. In the first place, I had been a daughter, the product of the lawful union between my mother and father. As sinful as my intentions may have been, I had always observed a certain piety, a childish reverence of convention, when it came to this union. I had no desire to supplant her, to take her place in the marital bed, to be anything other than the illegitimate ray of sunshine that brightened his workday afternoons. It was essential to me that Steadman was married, for it meant that—Byronic qualities aside—he was respectable; that he cared about appearances; that he hadn't spent the years before we met as a roving bohemian, moving from woman to woman. It meant that, by the time we met, his longing had been refined. It was the refined lust of an educated, dissatisfied man in his early forties: a lust that, I was convinced, could only be fulfilled by the likes of me.

RAINS CONTINUED throughout the first week of our relationship. I was in love with the sodden fields beyond the classroom windows, with the slick bricks and asphalt, with every silver droplet hanging from the eaves. My love was boundless. It encompassed everything, since everything was part of the same world as my love for him. Everything in the world seemed to reference our love. The azaleas on the path to the library were as full and red as his desktop chrysanthemums, as anything that opens or bleeds with desire. When I heard the rains, I couldn't help but think back to our midweek tryst in the locked classroom, and my own pearled stomach. I heard the rains and longed to be flooded.

I lost whole lessons in dreaming; dreams that differed from those of our courtship, since they were grounded in the rich stuff of reality—in the actual salt of his sweat, the actual dimensions of his manhood, the actual moans that I elicited from him, simply by being a young and beautiful receptacle. I gave thanks to the gods of interior design, to their unlikely penchant for doors that locked from the inside and windows that faced out onto the natural world, rather than into hallways where schoolgirls shuffled and lynx-like deputies prowled. When, at morning break, Marcelle waved a giggling palm in my face and snapped her cold-pinked fingers loudly, my only reaction was to beam.

"She's out of it," Amanda concluded snidely. "Totally out of it."

AFTER POSSESSING me that Friday, my lover drew me onto his lap and lavished me with praises and caresses, much as he had the last time we were together. I took advantage of this by posing a deliberate, female question. "You really think I'm beautiful?"

"More than beautiful," he assured me. "You're a work of art. You're a Pre-Raphaelite painting. In fact, I used to look at you reading by that window there and imagine you as Collier's *Lady Godiva*. Do you know John Collier?"

I shook my head.

"I'll have to show you the painting one day." He smiled his slightly uneven smile. "Danielle and I saw it when we were in England. The likeness is astounding. Never did I dream I'd be touching—"

"When," I cut in, more deliberately still, "did you realize that you were in love with me?"

"Oh, my darling, I wanted you from the start. The first time that I saw you, sitting under your laurel trees, looking just like Daphne . . ."

"Daphne?"

"Apollo's first love. A wood nymph. He pursued her and she turned herself into a laurel tree to escape. Actually, it was her father who transformed her. He was a river god. She begged him to let her remain a virgin and he obliged." Steadman laughed. "Fortunately for me, I've never had to worry about divine intervention. Have I, my Daphne?"

"No, never," I quietly agreed.

"Did you know," my master went on, looking into my eyes, "that Apollo was the god of poetry?"

"Apollo," I tried out the name, sensing that this was what he wanted, "My Apollo."

His expression, at that moment, could not have been more self-satisfied. I laid my head on his chest. I sighed. I told him that I too had been in love with him from first sight.

ALTHOUGH WE had only been lovers for a week, it felt as if I had been doing it for much longer, as if we had been rehearsing the same dialogue for centuries. I knew, by then, that it would never get any better for me; that it would always be bitter and painful and perplexing. I also knew that I was helplessly addicted; that I would go on doing it whether I wanted to or not, simply because I had to, and because it was the thing that was done. I was condemned to the repetition, to the mindless performance of a ritual that made little sense to me, and whose benefits shrank to nothing when pitted against the risk, the agony, the potential for disaster that attended our every coupling. I could only hope that it was a more pleasurable experience for him.

As I saw it, nothing could be simpler than the transports that he underwent, the radiant void that he inhabited, while I turned my face and attempted to predict where and how hard the next blow would fall. When it was over, perhaps, his feelings were not so simple. There was grief, guilt, and gratitude— an excessive kind of gratitude that made him take me onto his lap and whisper all kinds of praises and diminutives, which I blushed at receiving. At these times, I could ask him anything about himself and he would answer honestly; anything about myself, and he would answer in the most lyrical and hyperbolic of terms. The sweetness of the aftermath always had a palliative effect on me, contrasting as it did with the starkness of what had come before. I grew to depend on it, awaiting it as a forgetful mist that told me it had not been all terror, all agony.

In the week and a half leading up to Thanksgiving, we managed to make love on several more occasions. The usual times were established—Mondays and Fridays after school, Wednesdays during fourth period and lunch hour—as well as the usual techniques. For the time being, we wouldn't deviate much from these techniques.

Technicalities: he continued to use his *interruptus* method, whenever he could stand it; he continued to be on top; he continued to have me on the olive green carpet of his classroom—though we tried it on his desk as well. Non-technicalities: I continued to feel, to pine, and to suffer more than he could ever know; to give myself over to the pain for pleasures that were at best ambiguous.

There was a kind of pleasure in it—I don't deny that. Yet it wasn't the divine pleasure that I'd brought myself to expect. Some weeks ago, in a rare moment of seriousness, Marcelle had asked Amanda to describe what it felt like. "It's weird. You grow to like it, but it's weird. Like having an alien inside you." If I had to describe it, I would say that it was like learning to like a new kind of music by listening to the notes that weren't played, finding warmth and relief in the hollows, the vales between the mountains of dissonance. It was a dull, woeful, earthbound pleasure—not at all divine.

I came to him on the appointed days with a blend of girlish innocence and affected experience, which served to provoke him by undermining my innocence. I was still virginal enough that I desired to provoke him, without necessarily desiring the consequences of such provocation. One morning, I caught sight of a perfect red apple on the breakfast cart and snatched it up to put on his desk when we met that afternoon.

"Are you trying to bring about my fall?" he quipped, wistfully.

In answer, I gave an ironic half-smile and picked the apple up from where I had placed it, turning it about in my elegant white hands before touching its coolness to his lips. He bit in.

"I have tasted of the fruit," he announced, "Yet still, I am in paradise."

"Is it ripe?" I questioned.

"A little tart."

When he wasn't instructing me in the mechanics of love, he was instructing me in the poetics of it, seducing me mentally with the stories and words of great lovers whose tradition we were carrying on. There was the original, the myth, almost too sacred to mention, which prompted him to call me "my nymph, my Daphne," and to insist that I respond to him as "Apollo." In a former life, my lover had been a poet-god, pursuing me through the woods of Arcadia. Since then, his fantasies had been filled with green leaves and sun-dappled white skin. In the fourteenth century, I was incarnated again as a noble lady in a green dress, attending Easter service. The poet Petrarch glimpsed me and immortalized me as "Laura."

"Tell me some Petrarch," I asked him, knowing how eager he was to do so. He chose to recite his favorite three lines.

> *e non se transformasse in verde selva*
> *per uscirmi di braccia, come il giorno*
> *ch' Apollo la seguia qua giù per terra*

". . . 'and let her not transform into green wood/ escaping from my arms, as on the day/ that Apollo pursued her, down here on earth' . . ." he translated for me, once he was done showing off his Italian.

"Where did you learn Italian, anyway?"

"From my mother."

"Your mother was Italian?"

He nodded sagely. "Of Florentine stock. Like Dante, and the Medicis. Her name was Caterina."

"Is that where you got your daughter's name from?" I inquired thoughtlessly, then blushed as he gave me one of his sly, haven't-you-been-listening-closely looks. It wasn't the first time he'd caught me out, knowing more than I needed to.

"Catherine. Indeed." He went on, "My father was called John. He was a surgeon. He didn't know a word of my mother's tongue, and never tried to. Neither did my brother. I was always her favorite, because of that. She'd sit me in the kitchen and tell me all about Dad's *meretrices*."

"His what?"

"His whores." Steadman smiled roguishly. "Nurses, neighbor-women. It was nothing, really. He was always a ladies' man and she let herself go so quickly. She couldn't have expected him *not* to stray . . ."

I was careful not to question him too persistently about his origins, fascinating as they were, for fear that this would cause him to turn his attentions toward my own. In fact, he refrained from delving into my past with a stubbornness that suggested he already knew, or at least sensed, more than I would've cared to reveal. Did teachers have access to that sort of thing? I supposed that it was possible. I supposed it was also possible that the moral questionability of what he was doing with me made him squeamish about the subject of parents. Perhaps he preferred to imagine that I had been born out of the woodland and that his gaze gave me life, much in the same way as God breathed life into Adam.

I was more than willing to go along with this fantasy, to cast him in the role of poet-god, both lover and creator. In fact, since the beginning of my time at Saint Cecilia's, I'd gotten into the habit of thinking of myself as a kind of orphan; a father-born being who, cut off from her paternal origins, had every right to choose a new god. Considering the distance between my mother and myself, which was bridged only by biweekly phone calls and carefully contrived notes, it was relatively easy to maintain this illusion. I'd deliberately forgotten to inform her of the parents' weekend back in October and the parent-teacher conferences that were happening later that month (though, since things had started up between me and Steadman, part of me yearned to put her in the same room as the man who knew and worshipped every inch of my young body). As the holiday period crept closer, I was aware that I wouldn't be able to avoid reuniting with the woman for much longer. This apprehension was reinforced by her most recent letter, quoted in brief:

November 11, 2002

Carmel-by-the-Sea
Monterey County

Dear Laurel,

I'm so happy to hear that you're still enjoying school. Jill & Lee are still as kind as ever but that doesn't stop me from missing my darling daughter! They are begging me to stay for another weekend but I think its time for me to get back to the real world, don't you? Anyway, if I drive home on Thursday I can stop at your father's grave on the way to put some flowers down for his anniversary (can you believe it's already been 3 months??). I was thinking of buying some nice Lily of the Valley like we had at the service but let me know if you want something else . . . maybe some poppies or zinnias?

I feel dizzy when I think of all the boring business waiting for me at home. I've made some appointments next week with some of your father's lawyer-friends and that accountant whose daughter you went to Sacred Heart with (remember Mr. Wells?). I'm hoping to have everything sorted by the Wednesday though before I pick you up so we can have a nice, relaxing holiday together, just the two of us. There are lots of important things that I want to discuss with you, but don't worry—I won't be making any important decisions without talking to you first!

I'm counting down the days until Thanksgiving. Please call me when you get this letter or soon after.

Love Mommy

XOXOXO

P.S. I almost forgot to congratulate you on your grade for that English paper. Your father would be so proud!

She would be picking me up from boarding school on Wednesday, a half day, and keeping me with her until Sunday— a painful prospect. It was difficult enough talking to her on the phone, let alone in person. As for Steadman, I didn't doubt that he would be spending the holiday with his wife and children, playing the part of dutiful husband and father, just as I would be the dutiful, virginal daughter.

It therefore came as a shock to me when he announced on Wednesday, after class had broken and the others had gone off to pack, "Danielle and the children fly to Philadelphia on Friday. Can I pick you up in the evening?"

"What for?" I asked unthinkingly.

"For a weekend of passion, I should hope. Think about it: you'll be away from school; I'll have the house all to myself until Sunday . . ."

"What about my mother?"

"Make something up. Tell her you're staying with a school friend." He kneaded my shoulders through the thin cotton of my blouse. I was poised in his lap, wearing everything but my shoes and sweater. My mother wasn't coming until late afternoon, so we could take our time. "You're a clever girl; I know you'll find an excuse . . ." He said. He proceeded to kiss me, softly and at length.

It would break her heart, of course, but did I really care about that? Anyway, what was another pang of conscience to someone who was already living with more guilt than a single soul could handle? I placed my hands on his shoulders. I opened my eyes briefly to glance at his handsome face turned up toward my own. I was learning to enjoy his kisses, with their stale, coffee taste and strange refinements. I kissed him back until we were both quite breathless.

"I'll find an excuse," I told him, dabbing at my lips.

"That's my girl," said Steadman. His hands passed down from my shoulders to my hips. "You're a good girl, aren't you? You're a clever girl . . ."

"Yes, sir."

I KNEW that it was wrong to be making such arrangements, to be abandoning my poor widowed mother for a weekend of sin with Steadman. I knew that it was even more wrong for the sin to be taking place in the house he shared with his family; that I was overstepping the mark by agreeing to enter another woman's house, another woman's bed. My place was in the locked classroom, spread across the carpet that burned me or the desk that bruised me; I was the mistress, and had no right to the comforts of a married woman. By giving in to this particular request of his, I was surely laying myself open to torment—if only in the form of intensified feelings and the accompanying hope that I might actually have a future with him.

I consoled myself with the thought that I had no say in the matter; that I was completely in his thrall; that anyone unfortunate enough to love as I did would have acted the same way. It wasn't to be forgotten that the widow who I now pitied had once been in love; that she too had been feeble, sensuous; that I was merely following the example she had set for me. All the same, something pure and hardened in me told me that our sins weren't to be compared. What she had done in innocence, I did in cold blood, with full consciousness of its perversity.

His touch was still fresh on my body when my mother came to collect me that afternoon. Over the past three months, she had continued to dress in mourning—a Victorianism that I admired her for, even as I noted the way that it washed out her complexion and rejoiced in my own vermilion sweater, the cheerful flutter of my miniskirt. She remarked effusively on how grown-up I was looking, on how there had been a change in me. As we piled into the Peugeot, she concluded that my hair was longer.

That evening, we dined in Japantown. To prevent her from reminiscing about her time in Kyoto with my father, I steered the conversation toward Romantic poetry, telling her everything that I knew about Coleridge's drug habit, Shelley's revolutionary fervor, the scandalous love life of Lord Byron. I told her that I was thinking of majoring in literature at college.

"Literature! How nice." She took a sip of her sake and announced unexpectedly, "You know, I *am* glad you've gotten over your psychology phase."

"What's wrong with psychology?"

"Oh, well . . ." She waved her hand in the air. "All that overanalyzing. It frightens me a little bit."

To demonstrate, she gave an affected shiver. She went on:

"Besides, I don't think everything lies as deep as what they say."

"Well, maybe not for some people," I responded coolly, taking up my green tea.

My mother gave a vague, airy laugh, as if unsure whether I was joking and, if so, who the joke was on. "Shall I order some more sashimi?" she asked.

It wasn't until we got home, and after she had traded her black daywear for a black peignoir set—part grim reaper, part film-noir prostitute—that she sat me down to discuss the important things mentioned in her letter. Gathering her robe about herself, she looked up at the ceiling and commented on the emptiness of the house, the impossibility of her rattling around there on her own forever, with my father gone and me starting college in a year's time. She spoke of the beauty of Carmel-by-the-Sea, the hospitality of the Waldens—of Lee Walden in particular, who seemed to know everyone of importance and who'd been very encouraging of her talents as a decorator. She told me that it was only an idea, but that Lee knew of a beachside cottage whose owners were thinking of selling; that he could arrange an early inspection; that he and Jillian were more than willing to put us up for a few days over the winter. Lee himself was responsible for the landscaping of Arcady, which he counted among his best work: cobblestones, shadowed waters, pendulous wisteria. He had shown her photographs. It *had* to be seen. "It's your decision, sweetheart. I understand if you don't want me to sell the townhouse. I just thought it might be nice for us to take a look at this cottage . . ."

"It would be nice, Mom. I think it's a very nice idea."

THE FOLLOWING day, we had a modest lunch of turkey breast, string beans, and sweet potato. Despite its modesty, my mother cried on cue partway through the meal, lamenting the fact that my father wasn't with us at the table as he'd been the year before. I reminded her that he'd hardly eaten anything the previous year, that eating had been painful for him. At these words, she grew quiet, much as a child might between one storm of sobs and another. "He was a very sick man," she hiccupped. "Poor, poor Jonathon. He was a very sick man."

"He was very sick," I echoed and offered to refill her wine glass.

I was clearing the table and my mother was in the den, nursing her third glass of Pinot Gris, when I received the call from Mr. Steadman. I promptly stole outside to take it, settling on the porch steps and shivering from the late afternoon chill. Stained-glass windows glowed across the street like Chinese lanterns.

"Oh, I'm dying," he moaned into the receiver. "Tell me it's sorted. By this time tomorrow, I could be holding you in my arms."

"I'm working on it."

"Don't let me down, or I'll be rattling around all weekend like a lonely bachelor. Eating leftovers. Drinking all the wine in the cellar . . ."

I laughed. He really was a master of hyperbole.

When I returned to the den, I found my mother poring over old photographs and dutifully went to join her on the sofa. My father as a young graduate. My father as a young law clerk. My father as a young groom at their outdoor wedding, which she attended in strappy sandals and a garland of cherry blossoms. I was struck by how youthful my father was compared with Steadman and wondered whether I'd ever regret not giving myself first to an upright young man, with a trim waistline and an unwrinkled face.

There were far fewer pictures of him in middle age, though he remained handsome enough. The most recent were from Easter that year and had him unshaven, looking quite the roué with his two-piece suit and glass of red wine (the truth was, he couldn't have more than a couple of sips without it interfering with his medication). It gave me a peculiar feeling to see the shots in which I'd been asked to pose beside him in my white Easter frock, patterned with evil black flowers; to remember how anxious I'd been, and how I'd tried not to let my anxiety show when he placed an arm around my waist at my mother's bidding. I felt a similar anxiety as the lie stumbled past my lips. "Mom, my friend Catherine is touring St. Mary's College this weekend. She wants to know if I can come with her."

"Catherine who?"

"Catherine Steadman."

I WAS ready for him almost two hours earlier than I had to be, dolled up in a plum-colored dress and matching lipstick. Before dressing, I had spritzed myself liberally with my mother's French perfume: oriental spicy, with notes of plum, bay, citrus, jasmine, myrrh, and Lily of the Valley. My legs were sheathed in black pantyhose. On my feet, I wore high-heeled black Mary Janes.

It was well after five by the time he arrived at my doorstep, unshaven and dressed far more casually in jeans and his chocolate brown sweater. Though my mother and I answered the door together, he greeted her first. "Good evening! You must be Mrs. Marks."

"Lizzie," she smiled, accepting his hand.

"Hugh Steadman. As you can see, my daughter is *in absentia*. We told her she needed to have her room ready hours ago but, as usual, she left it right until the last minute." He laughed—a convincing display of parental cynicism—and glanced at me darkly. "I hope your own is more organized."

"Oh, Laurel has been dressed for hours! Darling, why don't you go fetch your bag from the den?"

I flounced away, face burning. When I returned with my bag, they were discussing art, as his eyes had apparently chanced upon the framed Klimt picture while following my figure down the hall.

"Have you been to the Belvedere Gallery?" he was asking her.

"I have! My husband and I were in Vienna a few years ago."

"Then you must have seen the Schieles too."

"I love Schiele!" she simpered.

It went on that way for what seemed like forever. At last, duly charmed, my mother kissed me farewell and closed the door behind us—though not without accepting his hand once more. He took my bag from me and, walking down the path, gave me an innocuous compliment. "Those are nice shoes. What do you call those?"

"Mary Janes."

Parked across the road was a silver SUV. I don't know what I'd been expecting, but the sight of it amused me: it was so family man, so bourgeois. He placed my bag in the trunk and helped me into the vehicle, holding the door open and his hand out. As soon as we were safely hidden behind the tinted windows, I melted into his arms. We were both flushed and tongue-tied when we broke apart, minutes later. He started up the engine. I adjusted my dress.

"Did you have to flirt with my mother so much?" I asked him coyly, once we were on the road.

"I wasn't flirting. I was being a gentleman."

"Do you think she's attractive?"

"I think she makes very attractive daughters."

As we drove north through Pacific Heights, I pointed out the public gardens that I used to pass through every day as a Sacred Heart schoolgirl, the street along which my old school had been located, and various mansions whose owners' daughters I was acquainted with. We cut through the Presidio and across the Golden Gate Bridge. From there on, it was all tunnels, hills, and forest. Night spread across the sky like the warmth of his hand resting on my thigh.

At last, he announced, far-off and sonorous as a dream pilot: ". . . Welcome to Larkspur." I shook off my reverie to peer out through the velvet-blue gloaming at a sycamore-lined street, full of sprawling bungalows and ranch-style family homes.

He pulled up in front of one of the bungalows. I couldn't tell what color it was in the failing light, but there was a trellis and picket fence. Without a word, he got out and walked around to the trunk, straining his neck to scan the sleepy street for onlookers. Satisfied that we were alone, he opened the passenger door. "Come out, my nymph."

I felt woozy as I stepped out of the warm, stuffy vehicle and tottered down the garden path ahead of him. Cradled in the darkness of the front porch, he slipped an arm around my waist and breathed hotly down my neck, scrambling to fit the key into the lock. He dropped his keys. He cursed under his breath and gave a sharp gasp of laughter. Gripping my waist tighter, he forced the key in and pressed me forward into the house.

The shadows in the hallway were long and sharp. I was as disoriented as a child waking up from a long sleep, but this didn't matter to him. The bedroom was upstairs and he wanted me in it.

Oak sleigh bed. Flowered Laura Ashley style spread. A wedding photo on the nightstand. A slice of mirrored wardrobe, partly open. A whiff of mothballs, lilac, another woman's perfume. He was kneeling at the foot of the bed. He was tugging at my tights. He was kissing my insteps, moving up my increasingly bare legs. As his mouth brushed my inner thighs, it dawned on me what he was doing. *Not that,* I thought. *Anything but that.* I squirmed. I giggled. I closed my knees around the back of his neck. He pressed on with his cool, over-refined tongue. I was about to cry out when the phone in the hallway shrilled, louder than I ever could have. He rose from his worship to answer it, giving me a tigerish glance as he leaned and paced and listened.

". . . A delay? Two hours? Oh, no, I wouldn't . . ." I sat up on my elbows, pressing my scrawny legs together as best as I could. He came and sat down beside me, pushing me back into a position of repose and caressing me artfully, even as he continued talking. ". . . Yes, I was just about to. Yes, I know where it is. Don't mind me, Danielle, I have everything I need . . ." I writhed quietly beneath his touch. "All right, call me tomorrow. Have a safe trip, my dear." He hung up and tossed the phone on the carpet.

"Nothing to worry about. A flight delay," he explained curtly; then, more tenderly, "Why don't you take off that dress? I like you better without it."

HE TOOK his time with me, drawing out my torture as he'd never been able to do during our brief classroom trysts. I was quite stupefied by the end of it, unable to account for the sensations that had passed through me, the utter break between my mind and body. He held me. The hair on his chest was matted. His chin was coarse, resting against my forehead. He was large and coarse and sweaty and male, regardless of the fact that he had read Petrarch. I was a soiled lily, limp in his arms, utterly lost to myself.

He was a man with appetites. Having satisfied his appetite for me, his cravings were far more mundane. He asked if I wanted some supper and, finding me unresponsive, said that there was no need for me to get up; that he could fix me a plate and bring it to me right there.

I watched him rise from the bed completely as he was. It still frightened me somewhat to see him undressed; to fathom the discrepancy between his full-blown, middle-aged manhood and the pale, frail, teen-aged beauty that I was accustomed to. He put on what was nearest at hand—his undershirt and shorts—and left me strewn beneath the sheets. Minutes later, unable to stand being alone with my lack of self, I tremulously dressed and padded downstairs to the kitchen.

I found him standing at the oak bench before a spread of leftovers, soberly sipping at a glass of red wine. "Hello, Laurel," he greeted me—all politeness, as if he hadn't just left me alone in his bed, in a state of utter desecration. "Would you like some wine?"

I nodded dreamily and sat on one of the kitchen stools, barelegged beneath his brown sweater and my crumpled plum dress. "Vintage 1985. I chose this just for you," he boasted, pouring me a glass of dark Merlot. Then, more bitterly: "'Vintage!' Imagine."

I didn't have the capacity to imagine, at that point. As he busied himself with the food, I took a sip of my wine. It tasted bitter, as all wine did to me, and went straight to my head, enhancing the warmth of my afterglow. I hadn't eaten since midday; nevertheless, it was only at his insistence that I took up a fork and began on the plate of cold turkey, yams, and cranberry sauce that he had lovingly prepared from the scraps of the day-old Thanksgiving meal lovingly prepared by his wife. It was the first time I'd eaten in front of him, and I was afraid that it might disillusion him to see me perform such a rudimentary action. I need not have worried.

"You eat so daintily. Like a bird." He regarded me with a smile partway through the meal. "Look, you even point your little finger."

"Deportment classes," I said with a dab of my napkin. This seemed to genuinely please and fascinate him, and a silly smile took over his features. I suppose he liked the thought of a room full of girls doing dainty things.

After we'd polished off our supper, we took the wine to the den and sank into the softness of the family sofa—a lumpy, pale thing that could've done with reupholstering. Draped over it was a reddish throw rug, which brought out the brick of the disused fireplace, the warmth of the mahogany floorboards and coffee table. On the table was a bowl of walnuts, an assortment of home and garden magazines, and a botany book. For my benefit, he opened the book at *Laurus nobilis*, Grecian laurel. I smiled and flipped the page over to California laurel. I was a New World nymph, after all.

Behind us, there was a wall of bookshelves crammed with novels, knickknacks (a jar full of foreign currency, a Venetian mask, a Pompeii medallion), and photographs of the faultless nuclear family: darkly handsome husband; fair, angelic wife; brown-haired boy and girl, born in the April of 1989—roughly four years later than myself. The walls were hung with Romantic landscapes, a dreamy William Blake watercolor, and Jacques-Louis David's *The Death of Marat*. Everything about the room seemed to betray a precarious yet unbroken balance between Steadman the bourgeois and Steadman the bohemian: the Steadman who lived comfortably and the Steadman who was willing to destroy his own comfort.

As I was thinking of the two Steadmans, praying that the balance would never be broken, he was laying the foundations for a second seduction. He offered me walnuts, topped up my wine glass every time I took so much as a swallow. He invited me to stretch my legs across his lap, applying many caresses to them as he moved from one topic to the next: commenting on how much nicer his sweater looked on me than it did on himself; asking me whether I had yet had a chance to read any Keats, who we would be starting on in class the following week; expressing mock disapproval when I inquired about who the man swooning in the bathtub was in Jacques-Louis David's famous painting. "You don't know Marat? What do they teach you at that school?"

"There's only one teacher who I listen to, and he has more important matters to instruct me in."

"Is that so? And who might this learned individual be?"

"Mr. Wolfstein, of course."

"I'll have you know," he puffed himself up, "that Albert Wolfstein is a flaming homosexual. He made a pass at me back when I first started teaching."

I laughed. "You're making that up."

"I swear. He caressed my hand while we were taking a smoking break near the willows. Just like this . . ." He trailed his fingers over the back of my own hand.

"You don't smoke."

"*Now* I don't. Danielle made me quit after my thirty-fifth birthday."

I liked the thought of him as a fresh-faced thirty-five-year-old almost as much as he seemed to like thinking of me in my childhood deportment classes. To keep on the subject, I asked him, "Do you like being a teacher?"

He shrugged. "I've never done anything else."

"Why didn't you become a professor? You're smart enough."

A momentary pall came over his features, making me regret my presumption. With typical smoothness, however, he was fixing me with a jaded smile in the next instant. "I'm not cut out to be an academic, you know that. Just like I wasn't cut out for medical school. I don't have the patience. Or the ambition. Besides . . ." He had lightened up his tone another notch or two. ". . . I much prefer the company of schoolgirls."

I CAN'T say when exactly he took me back to the bedroom. I do remember a lot of flirting, and a change in his looks when we got onto our second bottle of wine. On any other man, this change would've been quite ugly. His eyes were blood-shot, unfocused, and leering. His imperfect teeth were stained slightly red. I was suddenly conscious of the stubble on his jaw, his hairy limbs, and the extra weight around his midsection. "You look more like Dionysus than Apollo, tonight," I remarked naively.

"I can be whoever you want me to be."

All of this devolved pretty quickly. I sat on his lap, warm-breathed and light-headed, ready to get it over with right there and fade into the blackness of a wine-induced sleep. I reached past the waistband of his shorts. I felt heat, coiled hair, expansion. "Oh, you bad girl," he commented on my boldness. "You're a bad, bad girl. I'm going to have to put you to bed and teach you a lesson!"

My knees buckled as I stood up from the sofa. I was forced to lean on him for support, slurring all kinds of nonsense as we stumbled upstairs. "I'm not bad. I'm good. You told me I was good once. You told me I was clever . . ."

My point went unacknowledged as he led me to the bedroom. My eyelids fluttered shut. When they opened, I was completely undressed and he was leaning over me, fumbling to fit himself in. I closed my eyes again, giving myself up to the blind force of my intoxication.

I HAD never slept naked before and, like a lot of new things, I wasn't sure whether I enjoyed it. During the night, he had full access to my body, which he seemed intent on making use of, even in his sleep. I was caressed by too many hands, brushed by too many lips. I curled up on my side to escape them. I slept, yet I had no rest.

In the morning, which was really afternoon, he was prompt to possess me again, though the air was almost too stale to breathe and my flesh sorely in need of bathing. As soon as he was done, he permitted me to head to the shower, telling me that there were fresh towels in the cabinet and that I was welcome to the royal blue bathrobe hanging on the hook. Midway through my ablutions, he let himself into the en suite, grumpily mugged at his unshaven face in the mirror, and prepared an Alka-Seltzer. He looked in at me showering and left the room without a word, returning half an hour later from another part of the house with wet hair, smooth cheeks, sudsy earlobes, and a bathrobe that matched my own.

In his absence, I had taken the liberty of drifting around upstairs, examining the family portraits, the bric-a-brac and minor artworks that lined the halls. I looked into his son Cole's bedroom, a gloomy lair of closed curtains and crossed wires, with posters by M.C. Escher and a number of amateurish, Escher-esque drawings pasted along the walls. His daughter's chamber, the next room along, was comparatively conventional, boasting a shelf full of Jane Austen novels and a wall plastered with pinup hunks. There was a plush horse on her bed; a photo-collage above it of the healthy, plumpish, brown-haired, brown-eyed girl and her friends. I leaned in closer to inspect the photographs, eager to confirm the lack of resemblance between us, and experienced a minor shock. Among young Cathy's girlfriends—dressed in a soccer jersey in one snapshot, gothic black in another—was the spooky little sister of Karen Harmsworth, with her face full of freckles and husky-dog eyes.

I went back to the master bedroom to await Steadman and couldn't resist peering into the wardrobe he shared with his wife. Her shoes—dainty slingbacks and sensible slip-ons—were lined up at the base of the closet, below the hems of her neat pencil skirts, cocktail dresses, jackets, and twinsets. These came in colors like cream, beige, lilac, lemon chiffon, and pastel blue. Their textures were fine and soft: cashmere, lambswool, silk, 100 percent cotton. I didn't doubt that this clean grown-up woman would hate the state their bedroom was in, with its heavy, impure air and Laura Ashley quilt set in disarray. This notion filled me with a mix of pride and despair.

To escape these feelings, I closed her side of the wardrobe and opened his, losing myself in the familiar odors and textures of his shirts, his sweaters, his jackets, and his underwear, until I heard him padding down the hall. At this, I put an end to my snooping and busied myself with the bed linen in a sham display of domesticity.

"Don't bother yourself with maids' work, my Godiva," he said gruffly as he entered the room, drawing me away from the bed. "We're just going to mess it up again tonight. Let's have some breakfast."

Neither of us had cleared up the kitchen the previous night. He dumped the turkey carcass and piled our dirty dishes into the sink, halfheartedly telling me that he would get to them later. I sat on the same stool as I had at dinner and watched as he brewed the coffee, asking me whether I liked it with milk or sugar. "Two sugars, no milk," I instructed him. As I sipped my sweet, steaming black coffee from a mug patterned with banal Van Gogh sunflowers, he left his own milky coffee to cool on the countertop and made an excessive amount of toast. I disappointed him by choosing just a single charred slice, which I nibbled on dry and with little appetite. He slathered the remaining five slices in butter and marmalade, and dispensed of them with relative ease. He followed them up with a fresh fig.

He apologized for his behavior the night before, though didn't specify what it was he'd done wrong. I was also faintly ashamed and couldn't shake the feeling that we'd somehow gone too far, that I'd let him see and do too much in my intoxication. Taking pains to be tactful, he asked me whether there was anything special that I'd like to do that day—within the confines of the house, of course; he couldn't have the good people of Larkspur seeing him with a woman who was not his wife, a girl who was not his daughter. I told him that I'd like it very much if he could read to me, a request that seemed to please him. "We'll take some poetry out to the hothouse. You'll love it in there, my flower."

After finishing our coffee, we passed through the den, ignoring the empty wine bottles and the bookshelves that lined the walls. He informed me that all the best volumes were in his private study—a small, well-concealed room located just beyond the den. Upon entering, I remembered the prior evening's thoughts about the two Steadmans, bourgeois and bohemian, and knew at once which one the tiny room was devoted to. On one wall was a portrait of Byron in Albanian garb; on another, Rossetti's *Beata Beatrix*. Not one home-and-garden magazine was in sight. Instead, the shelves were stocked with English and Italian poetry, poets' love letters, and illustrated art books. On the desk stood a miniature of the Belvedere Apollo, a bust of Dante, and a canister of writing implements, including a genuine crow feather quill. Steadman the bohemian had created a hideout for himself within the family home: the perfect place for a lonely, overeducated schoolteacher to indulge his fantasies of poetic glory.

The writing desk looked out onto the backyard, a furnace of autumn leaves. I squinted outside, bristling when I felt the unexpected warmth of his lips on my neck, his arms binding my waist. "It's strange to see you in here," he murmured.

"Why?"

"This is where I do all my marking, not to mention all my thinking about you . . ."

He proceeded to tell me of how, in days past, he would break from duty to flip through his books on Pre-Raphaelite art—finding my image in the thin-armed virgins of early Rossetti, the diaphanous nymphs of Waterhouse, Collier's russet Godiva. He told me of how he'd dreamed of expressing his desire for me in verse, though never got further than a line or two before deferring to the works on his shelves. He invited me to select something from there and, recalling his frequent references to Dante, I reached for the Rossetti translation of *La Vita Nuova*. He approved of my choice. He slipped the thin volume into the pocket of his bathrobe and, taking my hand, suggested that we retreat to the garden.

THE BACK porch overlooked a sprawling lawn, which boasted a set of green-plastic furniture, a totem-tennis pole, plots of soil, and pruned flower bushes. He told me that the garden was always alive with color in the spring, when his wife grew golden daffodils, blue delphinium, and all manner of roses. It was November, however, and the backyard's main source of color was in the orange-brown leaves clinging to the sycamore tree I'd seen through the window of Mr. Steadman's study. Beyond this tree lay Mrs. Steadman's hothouse.

He ushered me into this humid paradise, which was overrun with hanging ferns, oriental lilies, orchids, and nymphaea in tubs of stagnant black water. He showed me some lilies that Danielle had won a prize for two years ago in a Marin County flower show. He reeled off the names of various aquatic blooms, smirking when he arrived at *Nymphaea pubescens*. "What do you think, my pubescent nymph?" He withdrew his hand from the water lily and transferred it to my shoulder.

"How does your wife find the time for all this?"

"Oh, she finds time for everything," he said dryly, though not without a hint of admiration. "Danielle isn't an idle thinker like you and I. She does things."

I didn't know whether to be insulted by his inclusion of me in the same category of idlers as himself. I soon brushed aside these qualms, however, preferring to admire the shimmer of perspiration on his brow and the chest hair peeking out from the front of his bathrobe. I could already feel myself being seduced by the excessive heat of the place, the beauty of the flowers. He sat himself down on an overturned plant pot. I settled at his feet and rested my head on his knees, as I'd longed to do during those dreamy Friday afternoons. He began on the Dante.

His voice, smooth and rich as ever, had its usual effect on me. I sighed. I fidgeted: sweeping my hair off my face, loosening the collar of my robe, and tugging at his leg hairs as if they were blades of grass. He noticed my affliction. Unable to maintain that old façade of pedagogic detachment, he asked me in a low, shamefully obvious tone, "Are you feeling hot, my darling?"

"Are *you*?" My own tone was wry, critical. I slid my hand up his leg and, before he could answer, was groping in the darkness beneath his robe.

He responded as any man would, inhaling sharply and snapping the book shut. When he could no longer bear the teasing kisses I placed along his kneecaps, he threw open his robe, exposing his ugly nakedness and taking my head in his hands. I had known what I was getting myself into. Nonetheless, I wasn't quite prepared for the stifling act he had me perform—an act made more unbearable still by the thick, hothouse air.

When we emerged, all color had ebbed out of the afternoon. We retired to the bedroom once again, where we lay together for some hours in that twilit land between one climax and another. Given all the time in the world, we probably would've gone on that way, chafing, disassembling, and assimilating each other to no end. It had gotten to the point where I wanted it as much as he did; where I could no longer distinguish between his desire for me and my desire, between the pleasure he took in me and the pleasure of my subjection.

Of course, our time together was limited. I knew our time was almost over when we got up to order takeout, though we'd make love twice more before bed. The weekend was almost over, and it would never be the same again. I'd never be so free with him again, nor, going back to that life of locked classrooms and scheduled couplings, would I ever be satisfied with what I had.

I woke the next morning earlier than he did to cramps and soreness and a familiar, fetid dampness between my thighs—made foreign by my nakedness and by the man sleeping facedown at my side. I looked between the covers. I saw my own blood spotted on the sheets and was filled with horror, a mounting hysteria that couldn't be explained by the simple misfortune of suffering my monthly curse in another woman's bed. I touched myself. I saw blood on my hands and began to sob, as I hadn't sobbed since he first deflowered me. I sobbed and shook him awake, telling him that we had to clean up; that I was dirty; that she would know that I'd been in her house, in her bed. I told him that we had to wash the sheets; that we had to air out the room; that she would smell me; that I was sorry, so sorry.

That afternoon, he drove me back to school, wearing a clean dress and one of his wife's sanitary napkins. The main parking lot was crowded with parents and students, all of whom seemed to have arrived back at the same time, and were in no hurry to clear the area. He reversed, taking me instead to the smaller lot on the other side of campus, between the athletic fields and the performing arts center. There, he told me that he loved me, but that we'd been reckless; that it was sheer luck that I hadn't fallen pregnant that month; that we needed to establish new methods and, moreover, to be careful about how we behaved at school. I listened, damp-eyed, as he lectured me on the importance of keeping things under control so we could continue enjoying ourselves; of his unwillingness to become a father again, at his age. I dried my tears and gave him my cool cheek to kiss, retrieving my bag and stepping out of the vehicle without a word of agreement or protest.

THE FIRST weekend that he could get away from his family, and I from the loose supervision of the school grounds, he picked me up in the SUV and drove me to a clinic—a place where he was sure that they wouldn't ask too many questions. He gave me a wad of cash and waited in the car as I went inside, returning forty minutes later with a small paper package.

"Did you get what you need?" he asked tensely.

I nodded and patted the package in my lap.

"Good girl." He patted my hand, an echo of my previous gesture. He started up the car and, with forced casualness, began: "I saw a motel a little way back. Or we could just park somewhere quiet; there were some nice oaks . . ."

"Oaks, please."

"Anything for my wood nymph," he smiled, backing out of the parking lot.

PART FOUR

Since the beginning of our affair, my grades had suffered slightly, as had my ability to concentrate in classes other than Mr. Steadman's. Despite this, I felt that my mind had never been more fertile, my daydreams never more rich with possibilities. I neglected my textbooks in favor of the titles he presented me with, which I read through diligently and devotedly, underlining the phrases that seemed to express something of our love. I kept these phrases in mind, wrote them down, or repeated them to him while he held me in his lap, stroking my bare legs or running his fingers through my hair. I was eager to uphold the intertextual nature of our affair.

December was low clouds, the late honey of afterschool lovemaking by the classroom windows. We were so high above everything and the grounds so windswept that we didn't have to worry about being seen. He would leave me as late as five forty-five on some Mondays and Fridays, stomach growling as he fixed his wristwatch and mumbled about the Hispanic cleaning women who carried keys and came at six. If the hallways were empty enough, we'd sometimes share a kiss outside his door. Usually, however, I'd slip out before him, walking prettily for his benefit and exchanging glances with the last stragglers carrying instruments up from the performing arts center. If we were especially late, I might lock eyes with one of the squat cleaning ladies, rolling along with her blue smock and vacuum.

There were inconveniences, of course. The Friday when, after circling the humanities wing, I came back to find him talking Shelley with bespectacled Emma Smith, who couldn't risk another B minus. That other Friday when his daughter called needing a lift somewhere, while I kneeled topless on the carpet, cupping my just-unhooked bra to my chest. The Monday when he was held up an hour and a half by a staff meeting and had to make love to me hastily before the cleaners came—telling me he'd make it up to me later, as he zipped up and smoothed down his trousers. I dealt with these vexations bravely, fatalistically, never letting him see the way my soul sank with every wasted minute of our love.

At the end of December, before we parted ways for Christmas, he made me a present of Petrarch's *Canzoniere*, the inside of which he inscribed as follows:

Bella Mia—

> *These sonnets were not written, as you may think, by the Italian bard Petrarch for his Laura, but by a generous and noble seer who foresaw my love for you all those centuries back and had the benevolence of putting it into words for me—knowing that the mere sight of you on your knees in your green bower would render me incapable of speech. My girl, may all leaves burn, may all temples be defaced, may all poetry fall to ruins, as long as you remain forever Laurel, Laurel, Laurel, my green, my glory!*
>
> > *Ardently yours,*
> >
> > *Hugh*

I thanked him graciously, though there was a certain hypocrisy about such exalted words coming from the man who, only a quarter of an hour ago, had gotten me to kneel beneath his desk and do for him what I'd done that day in the hothouse. The knowledge had begun to dawn on him that he could use me in more ways than the traditional, that beyond my initial decorum, I was more than willing to be exploited. I came to relish the plush feel of his glans beneath my tongue, the throbbing of his dorsal veins, his salty taste surging into my open mouth. I loved how harassed and exposed he made me feel, bending me over his desk and tugging down my tights to enter me from behind. Perhaps my favorite thing, however, was to be held in his lap, my legs straddling his torso and my face to his. In this position, I felt utterly safe, small.

He was teaching me how to please and I was learning quickly, shedding more of my inexperience by the day. Instinctively, however, I knew the qualities he wished me to retain: that way I had of lowering my eyes when faced with the brute fact of his manhood; my tendency to hide my face in the crook of his neck when crisis was approaching and for minutes afterward; my unwillingness to talk about anything we did or the body parts involved in doing it, except in the vaguest terms— "love," "you," "me," "inside," "here," "this." I deferred to his large hands, his smooth instructions, his twenty-five years of additional experience.

Overall, my Steadman was a vigorous lover, an enthusiastic lover, a lover who I suspected thought himself better than what he was, but was no less appealing for this conceit. He was a lover with experience and arts, which he employed offhandedly, as if believing that what worked for one woman could be applied to any other. He had the amusing habit of breaking off from these arts abruptly, however, whenever his own physical state became a serious concern. It was no secret to me that my pleasure was secondary; that after him came the flood; that, when he used his fingers or tongue on me, it was only to be artful, to add a patina of refinement to the violent act of possession. It was a wonderful, terrible thing to be loved as he loved me—so vigorously, so brutally and, at the same time, with such intelligence, such refinement!

Each morning, I took a pill for him, which prevented any life from growing inside my young womb, no matter how often or how strenuously he had me. It happened on average about three times a week: three times a week from November until halfway through June, with allowances for vacations and monthly restrictions. In total, we must've been together almost a hundred times—a hundred times without his seed taking root within me, without my girlhood being burdened with a woman's responsibilities, without my body changing. I could never allow myself to change, to digress from the mythopoetic perfection that he'd bestowed on me, and this was my greatest anxiety as we burned through that winter.

For all his appetites, Steadman's aversion to women at times seemed to equal my own. I remember one afternoon not long after his staff meeting when I broached the issue of Miss Kelsen's blue-eyed, dimpled, soon-to-be-wedded prettiness. "You mean Suzanne? Oh, she's lovely now. But you can just tell that she'll be pregnant in a year and, after that, it will all go to hell," he responded, more bitterly than necessary for a man simply wishing to dispel his mistress' jealousy. I was so taken aback by this judgment that I decided to interrogate him further. "What about the girls in class, do you think they're pretty?"

"Which girls?"

"Amanda?"

He made a face. "She's cheap."

"Christina?"

"Too plump."

"Karen? Or Emma? Or Maryanne. . . ?"

"Unexceptional. You know they can't even be compared to you."

"What about Kaitlin Pritchard?"

"Who?" He feigned ignorance, blanking his face of all expression.

"She isn't in our class, but you've met her. She knows your wife. I heard she went to your house for dinner once."

I had him there. He looked uncomfortable for a moment, then made a show of remembering. "Oh, *her*. Well . . . I wouldn't kick her out of bed. But she's nothing I haven't seen before. Just a younger Danielle."

"Your wife is pretty. I'd be glad to look like her when I'm older."

"You don't even need to think about getting old, my nymph." He smiled condescendingly. "Believe me, you have a long time to go until you're Danielle's age . . ."

WHEN MY mother asked me what I wanted for Christmas, I requested some cute underthings, dispelling her curiosity by telling her my old ones were all worn out and that I may as well replace them with something nice. As usual, we didn't have a proper tree—only an indoor bamboo plant, which neither of us put much effort into decorating. Nonetheless, we attended Midnight Mass as we did every Christmas Eve. Before Christmas lunch, we traded parcels.

I had mounted and framed one of my best Japanese inkings for her, showing the willows and the lake. As for my mother, she'd more than delivered on my request, giving me a selection of lacy things from her favorite French boutique off Fillmore Street. "Thank you, Mom." I kissed her on the cheek and tried not to look suspiciously overjoyed. "You didn't need to spend so much."

She waved away my concerns. "You're old enough for nice things now. Just make sure you hand-wash these. This is Chantilly lace, honey . . ."

I spent the remainder of Christmas break putting the final touches on my college applications, attempting to make up for my lack of extracurriculars—sleeping with teacher, alas, did not count—by dazzling the gods of admissions with my precocious knowledge of art and literature. At my behest, my lover had furnished me with a letter of recommendation, which painted me up, in glowing terms, as one of the most gifted young women that he'd ever encountered in his ten years at S.C.C.S. Moreover, in a fit of passion, he'd promised me whatever grades I wanted for all my upcoming assignments. This promise didn't mean much, considering I was already getting straights As in English.

He effused that I had a bright future ahead of me, that I could be anything that I wanted to be, and that I'd get into any school I set my sights upon. "I can imagine you as a Bryn Mawr girl," he smiled when I reeled off the list of colleges outside my own state that I was applying to. To my disappointment, however, he didn't remark upon my penchant for schools in the state of his birth. Worse still, he didn't make any reference to how our relationship would be continued, post-graduation.

As intense as my attachment to him was, I couldn't allow myself to consider the possibility of him leaving his wife for me. In fact, if we were to carry on making love once I ceased being his student, it would have to be on a far more sporadic basis—a truth that struck me as too dire to contemplate. The clean break of life in another state was almost preferable to the prospect of a prolonged affair, with me as a student at some Californian liberal arts school. Of course, neither option was even as remotely desirable to me as the self-destructive fantasy of foregoing college altogether and living as a kept woman in a hideout of his choosing.

Between bouts of productivity, I refrained from thinking about my future, hoping that my fate would somehow be decided for me. I lay on the daybed reading the *Canzoniere* as my father's books and papers were gradually cleared from the room. Now and then, a spasm of longing would force me to set my book aside and press my thighs together, as isolated memories of our couplings flashed through my mind. I had become physical, dreadfully physical, under his regime.

My father's desk was cleared. My father's bookshelves were cleared. My father's wardrobe and medicine cabinet were cleared. My mother was keeping herself busy to avoid thinking about the tragedy of our first Christmas without him. "Do you want any of these?" she questioned me at one point, still dressed in her widow's weeds and carrying a pile of philosophy books out of the room. "No thanks," I replied, barely looking up from Petrarch's sonnets. She stopped in her tracks to look at me quizzically. "Where did you get that book, sweetheart?"

"San Rafael," I responded coolly.

"Can I see? That looks like an antique."

"Later." I flushed, thinking of Steadman's inscription. "I'm reading now."

She had other questions too. "Why so many schools in Pennsylvania?" was one of them, which I dealt with by citing the superior number of liberal arts colleges in that state. "Is that all your father's pills?" she asked another day, showing me the box of prescription medicines that she'd collected from around the house. This collection didn't include the bottle of muscle relaxants I'd stolen all those months ago and now kept in a private compartment of my toiletries bag, along with my dial of birth control pills. "Have you met any nice boys?" was repeated more than once over the course of my stay, always in a syrupy tone. I never dignified it with anything more than a noncommittal shrug or a typical teen-aged eye-roll.

Toward the end of break, while my mother was out, I went to the en suite bathroom to admire myself in my new lingerie. I turned. I preened. I posed. I located my parents' bathroom scales and expected the number on the dial to conform with my self-esteem. Instead, I suffered an unpleasant surprise. Since September, my weight had gone up an entire three pounds; not much, perhaps, in the scheme of things, but a travesty for a girl who ate as little as I did and had formerly monitored herself from one day to the next. When I inspected my half-naked form, it seemed that everything—my breasts, my belly, my backside—had grown more curved. To my own eyes, I was suddenly as grotesquely voluptuous as a Hottentot Venus. I wanted to weep my weight in tears, to never touch another morsel.

"I don't want any dinner," I told my mother as she was deciding what kind of pasta to cook that evening.

"Oh, Laurel." Her face fell. "Not this again."

"It's nothing. I just don't feel very well."

"Are you sure? You know how I worry about you starving yourself . . ."

"I'll have something when I'm feeling better. I just don't think I can keep anything down tonight."

"All right, honey, if you say so." My mother palmed my forehead and frowned at some imaginary fever or lack thereof. "It's probably from being cooped up with your books all week. All this stale air—it's not healthy. And your father's study is the worst. I don't know how you can stand sitting in that room day after day . . ."

I didn't bother telling her that sitting in that room was easy for me. She wouldn't have understood that what was hardest for me was the simple fact of changing, of enduring change.

On the first day of winter term, Marcelle skipped ahead of me while I was making my way to French class.

"Ger-man-yyy! Tell us about Ger-man-yyy!"

Amanda was with her as usual, looking at me with cool, amber eyes. Her gaze reminded me of the lie I'd told eons ago about spending Christmas with my fictive father in Trier.

"It was cold," I said simply.

"Did you eat any bratwurst?"

For a moment, I thought she was referencing the extra three pounds I was carrying. Thankfully, common sense interceded in time to tell me that this was just Marcelle's usual crude brand of humor.

"I ate *so* much at Christmas," Amanda complained, falling into step with me. "I'd better be careful. They say it's even harder to lose weight when you're on the pill."

"What?"

"Well, that's what I've heard."

"I mean . . . when did you start using it?" I tried to look unfazed, compassionate.

"God, you're out of it. Last month. My sister helped me get the prescription. Of course, my parents know nothing about it . . ."

I didn't know what pained me more to think of: the fact that the pill keeping me without child could also be slowing down my metabolism or the fact that I was now as sexually active as Amanda. Sitting in French class, I was so preoccupied with this question that I didn't hear the one Madame Rampling addressed to me.

"*Qu'est-ce que vous avez fait en vacances, Laurel?*"

She repeated the query, pursing her lips as I groped hopelessly for a reply. All eyes were upon me as I fumbled, Amanda's included, telling me exactly how far I'd fallen.

I DIDN'T go to him with my concerns about my body, just as I didn't go to him with my concerns about our future. Instead, I took it upon myself to make cuts at suppertime, and to suppress the thoughts that pained me most. Back in his arms that afternoon, I did everything as before—clinging to his neck and dulling my mind to all that lay ahead. He uncovered the new lace beneath my school uniform and smirked, "This is nice." It was defiled within the hour.

We had agreed to tone things down in class after our weekend together, which suddenly seemed to me like a distant paradise, an age of innocence that I'd never get back to. As before, he spent most lessons reading to us from the front of the room; when he did come by, however, he made sure to divide his time equally between each desk and to address me and Marcelle together—something he'd done in the early days of our romance, before he knew me well enough to engage me separately. In this way, I came to find myself listening, chin in hand, as he recited snippets of Keats or responded to some query of Marcelle's. I mostly stayed silent, taking note of the ties that he wore, of his cologne and the salty, manly musk that underlay it. I took note of how his hair fell over his brow, how long it had been since he last shaved, and a thousand other details of his nearness. I'd then match these details up with my memories as a fond lover: learning how to do a half-Windsor knot with his maroon tie; brushing my lips against the one-day stubble of his jaw; running my hands through his soft, dark chestnut hair, which showed no signs of thinning and only the rarest strand of silver. Now and then, I'd feel compelled to keep him there longer by asking him to explain something complicated. One day, I got him to stay for a full fifteen minutes talking about negative capability.

When it was time for us to start on William Blake, Mr. Steadman deviated by spending the better part of a lesson showing us the poet's illustrations for Dante's *Inferno*. He spoke of the lovers' whirlwind, where the souls of those condemned for lust were blown about endlessly; of the wood of suicides, where sinners were caged in bark like Ovid's nymphs. In the dimness of the classroom, with only the projector screen for illumination, his features were obscure. His intonations seemed to come from a deeper, more distant place, lulling me with the inevitability of my punishment.

Out in the hallways, he could still be seen walking alongside Mr. Wolfstein, Mrs. Poplar, and less frequently, Miss Kelsen. I passed him by without appearing to pay heed, though the mere sight of him had me itching with desire, nerves, and compunction over our most recent couplings. The physical evidence of these couplings was always increasing. After he gave me a large reddish-purple love bite, I was forced to powder my neck and wear my hair down over my throat for a full week. Undressing in the locker room, smaller bites could be observed at my clavicle, my ribcage, and my hipbones, as well as more enigmatic scrapes and bruises from the classroom carpeting and furniture. One morning early in February, I woke up to find myself afflicted with my first ever cold sore.

Weeks later, the same sore appeared at the side of Steadman's mouth. I almost yearned for someone to take notice, to put two and two together, to see how the corruption of one lover was echoed in the other. Out of a similar impulse for sabotage, I would sink my teeth into his torso and suck until the blood pooled beneath his skin, until the vessels burst and he pushed me away, laughing that I was hurting him like a veritable lamia. I was proud of the bruises I left on him, which matched my own, and which he was forced to wear like badges of his infidelity, going home to his wife. Likewise, I was thrilled by the prospect of my scent—my warm, acrid, unmistakably youthful scent—announcing itself to her whenever they lay down at night. As much as I shied from the thought of him actually telling her anything, throwing away his marriage for a future that I had trouble contemplating, I wanted her to sense my physical claim on him. I wanted her to know that, though their lives were bound in every other respect, his flesh was mine.

Three times a week, I'd be anointed with his fluids—fluids that had their origins in the knotted system of ducts and glands inside him, and that came out smelling mysteriously of chlorine. On Wednesdays, when we habitually made love during lunch hour, I would bring this smell with me to history class and dwell in its alkaline dankness as Mr. Henderson's chalk scraped on the blackboard and Kaitlin Pritchard's lovely neck hovered before me. It was plain to see that I was no longer pure, that I was tainted in more ways than the fastest girls at school. Nevertheless, it all took place without comment. Nobody cared enough to acknowledge my contamination.

UNLIKE MY spiritual decline, my academic decline was acknowledged. Before winter break, a special assembly was held for twelfth-graders, where the phenomenon of "Senioritis" was addressed. Mrs. Faherty, trembling with indignation at the thought that any S.C.C.S. girl could be willing to endanger her future prospects (and the school's reputation), called up a procession of witnesses. There was a tragic character called Donna Sibley, an ex-student whose acceptance into Berkeley had been rescinded when she got a D in AP history. There were department heads, who spoke of the scores of bright students they'd seen letting their grades slip as soon as their college applications were in. There was the school psychologist, Dr. Lisa Bakewell, who invited us all to drop by for a chat if we ever had trouble coping. Finally, there was Kaitlin, who gave a pep talk about the virtues of supplementing study with wholesome social activities and exercise—all the while tossing her golden hair and shifting her weight from one long leg to the other.

The whole thing was a farce, redeemed only by scenic views of Steadman. He sat on the podium in a purely decorative capacity next to Mr. Wolfstein, looking bored and slightly haughty. At one point, he said something behind his palm to Wolfstein, causing the older man to convulse with silent mirth. My lover, it seemed, was something of a comedian.

We were only able to eye each other from afar, shuffling out of the auditorium: Steadman, talking with his hands while keeping in step with bearded Mr. Wolfstein; me, turning my head to look at him as the crowd carried me off in a swell of gray and tartan. From there, it was straight to second-period math class, where Mr. Slawinski grilled us for an hour with equations. As we were clattering out for morning break, he made an announcement.

"Not so fast. Libby Cloud, Laurel Marks, Ella Massie, Maryanne Rhymes, Jenny Smith . . . I'd like you to all stay back a minute."

There was a collective moan and exchange of eye-rolls. We settled back behind our desks, crossing our legs and cupping our chins in our hands. He remained standing, short and utterly sexless with his pocket pen and striped necktie. With a pang, I thought how much better my Steadman looked in chino pants.

"As you may know, the five of you scored below the class average in your latest test. In light of this morning's assembly, I think you could all benefit from a few hours of extra tuition. How does Tuesday afternoon sound?"

It didn't end there. In French class, Madame Rampling called us up individually to discuss how we might improve our proficiency in the language. "Laurel, you have a wide vocabulary and a good understanding of French grammar, but I feel you lack confidence in speaking and aural comprehension. Have you heard about the French conversation group after school? You can't make it on Mondays? *Quel dommage.* Perhaps you would like to borrow some cassettes. . . ?" Meanwhile, before last period, I received a memo from Dr. Bakewell recommending that I pay her a visit. I promptly tore it up.

That afternoon, entering Steadman's classroom for our first tryst of the week, I unpinned my hair and told him of my woes.

"Your mind is too beautiful to be wasted on mathematics," he declared. "Or on high-school psychologists, for that matter."

HE WAS due to turn forty-three at some point between the twenty-eighth of February and the first of March. It didn't matter when exactly: either way, the event fell during winter vacation, the better part of which I'd be spending down at Carmel-by-the-Sea with my mother. On Saturday morning, she would pick me up from Saint Cecilia's and drive straight down to the Waldens' cottage, Yellow Leaf. That same day, Lee Walden would take us to inspect Arcady, the cottage he'd described to my mother. Lately, she'd been raving about this cottage to me over the phone and in her letters.

I told Steadman about my plans with the greatest indifference, remarking that I was only sorry to be passing the week so far from him. As an afterthought, I added, "And now our ages will be further apart too. Twenty-six years."

"Oh, don't remind me," he groaned. "I'm well aware of how bad this would look, in a California court."

"'Statutory rape.'"

"'Corruption of a minor.'"

"'Criminal congress.'"

"'Unlawful carnal knowledge.'"

"How many years, do you think?" I asked, only partly in jest.

"Five, six years. Maybe less on probation."

"I'd visit you," I ventured.

"You'd better." He laughed. "It could be worse. Peter Abelard was castrated for bedding Heloise."

I'd been given the love letters between Abelard and his nineteen-year-old pupil earlier in the month, and was amused by a perceived similarity between Abelard's smug, cultivated tone and that of my teacher. This tone was something I also found in Byron, who—beyond the mood swings, the hot blood, and the indiscriminate appetites—seemed to me quite a cold character: the epitome of the rational, hypocritical male. Naturally, I was attracted to this. Nevertheless, it didn't escape me that such men had a habit of turning their women hysterical: Heloise continuing to be plagued by lust as an aging nun in her convent, Lady Caroline Lamb starving herself and running around London dressed as a pageboy.

It was Lady Lamb who inspired me to make him a special gift before we parted at the end of the week. In class, he'd told us a salty story about how Lord Byron's craziest girlfriend had once enclosed her pubic hair in a love letter. After bathing and perfuming myself the night before, I took out my nail scissors and made a clipping from my own delicate brown triangle. This was placed in a green marbled envelope, along with a note that I'd been agonizing over all week.

> LAUREL STEADMAN
> NEXT TO LAURA DEAREST
> & MOST FAITHFUL—GOD BLESS YOU
> OWN LOVE—RICORDATI DI DAPHNEA
> FROM YOUR CALIFORNIA NYMPH[2]

---

2. Lady Caroline Lamb to Lord Byron (1812):
   Caroline Byron
   next to Thysra Dearest
   & most faithful—God bless you
   own love—ricordati di Biondetta
   From your wild Antelope

"Perfect! It's perfect," he effused when I handed it to him. "And, of course, I will remember Daphne. I could never forget Daphne."

"Or Laura?"

"Or Laura."

"Or Lady Caroline?"

"Or Lady Caroline."

"Or Heloise?"

"Or Heloise. Let them castrate me; I'll never forget my Heloise."

I WAS in a pleasant if languid state of mind, making the two-and-a-half-hour trip south the next morning in the passenger seat of my mother's Peugeot. She still wore mourning. She had packed a suitcase full of elegantly mournful clothing, including a bathing suit of black nylon. For all this, her conversation was far from gloomy. She told me of the scandalous amount of money that our neighbors, the Pratchetts, had spent adding another turret to their Châteauesque monstrosity. She asked me if I recalled my father's colleague, Alan Hancock, and informed me that he was leaving his wife of fifteen years for a grad student. "Poor Jemima. I must go see her when we get back," my mother frowned—practicing, rather than expressing sympathy for the other woman's plight. Prematurely widowed, it was a plight she'd never have to suffer through.

It was after midday when we arrived at Yellow Leaf. We were greeted at the door by Lee and Jillian Walden, along with a fat old spaniel, which plodded up to me and sniffed my ankles at length. "What a terrible bruise you have on your leg, Laurel!" Jill gushed over a bit of Steadman's handiwork. I told her that it was nothing, merely an injury from gym class. Lee grinned a large-toothed grin and, with some swagger, offered to take our bags to the guest bedroom. "I'm afraid you'll have to share, girls! Josie is getting in from Pomona tonight."

"Josephine! How nice." My mother glowed, responding favorably to that "girls." "We don't mind sharing a room, do we, Laurel?"

In fact, I could think of few things I wanted less than to share a room and, as the case had it, a bed with my mother. All the same, I was a well-bred young lady and could put up no objections. At Jillian's invitation, I followed my mother and herself out to the patio, to take some post-travel refreshments.

"Cake, Lizzie? Laurel?"

"Oh!" My mother leaned forward to better inspect Jillian's offering, then bit her lip modestly. "Just an itty-bitty slice for me."

"Laurel?" Jillian gave me a sly look, her knife poised over the cheesecake. "It's *very* good."

"No, thank you."

"You can certainly afford it," she said teasingly, with a maternal cinch of my waist. Jillian herself was a short, fat-bottomed woman with a disproportionately long neck and a head full of sleek, dark hair.

"Jill can't afford it, but she still puts away more than all of us." Lee slouched out from the house, crossing the deck and setting his trim, stonewash-jeaned behind on the arm of his wife's chair. He gave her a genial, faintly condescending pat on her thick thigh. "Don't you, my dumpling? Actually, I think I might have some of that . . ."

With only a touch of sadness, the woman lowered her small, indistinctly colored eyes and cut him a wedge of cheesecake. He took up the plate, remaining spryly poised on the arm of her chair, his legs in a constrained figure-four. Lee was a tallish, tannish, fit forty-something-year-old with an all-American look about him: rolled-up sleeves, oversized white teeth, square jaw, and wavy once-blond hair. For all this, I found him repellent.

"Are you *sure* you don't want any, Laurel? Just a little slice like your mother's?" Jillian insisted.

I shook my head.

"She's worried about gaining weight," my mother said in the stagy, catty manner that parents use with other parents.

"I've gained three pounds," I defended myself lamely.

"I can't see where. In hair, probably," Jillian reached for my tumbling locks. "Her hair *has* grown since the funeral, hasn't it? Look at it. She's like that painting. You know, that Pre-Raphaelite one of the girl with all the red hair. Lizzie, help me out?"

My mother shrugged helplessly, showing her pale wrists and licking the crumbs from her fork. Lee gave her an appraising glance. "They both are. Regular Pre-Raphaelites."

I scowled at his misuse of Steadman's terminology and took a sip of my black coffee.

Later that day, Lee drove my mother and me around town in his convertible: pointing out cypresses and famous residences while expounding—ostensibly for my benefit—on the virtues of living in such a historically and artistically rich community. For my mother's benefit, he referred to the two of us collectively as "girls" or "young ladies," and talked endlessly of architecture: drawing her attention to the echoes of Antoni Gaudí in this or that Carmel cottage; speaking of the treasures of Barcelona, and pronouncing the city's name, to my disgust, with an affected lisp. Despising his pomposity, I stared out the window until we arrived on the doorstep of Arcady.

The owners had flown to Greece for the winter, leaving a key in Lee's possession. He ushered us inside with hushed exclamations about the quality of the redwood flooring, the exposed beam ceilings and the distribution of light. As the adults wandered from room to room, studying the architectural features, I could see my mother's mind working, imagining which of her *objets d'art* could be transferred to this comparatively rustic setting.

Bored of interiors, I strayed out to the gray-cobbled, mossy, shadow-plunged back garden. I descended from the porch to a pergola, overgrown with pendulous pink and purple wisteria. I ran my fingers through the soft, trailing blooms. I spied a series of verdigrised bronze nymphs and, further into the garden, a gloomy green pool, deeper than it was wide. At the far side of it was a slanted willow, casting strange shadows over the depths.

I crouched on the gray cobblestones and dipped my pale hand into the greenish pool water. It was cold yet clement to the touch. Unthinkingly, I pressed my dripping digits to my lips. I tasted salt and chlorine; Steadman. Head-swimmingly, half-swooningly, I raised myself from the poolside to squint at the glaring white sky. Below it, the roof was gray and shingled. The second-story window gaped open, exhaling white drapes. I heard a buzzing. I looked down to the white-framed pergola and perceived, hidden amongst the wisteria, a festering hornets' nest.

THAT EVENING, we sat out on the Waldens' patio, awaiting their daughter's return. The adults were drinking wine, which I was permitted as well, being almost eighteen and in the company of affluent liberals with European aspirations. I accepted a glass of red, hoping that it would alleviate something of my boredom. While it did take some of the edge off, however, it also induced a pang of longing, as I recalled that night on Steadman's sofa back in Marin County.

As the adults talked, I dreamed and drank, and occupied myself feeding a handful of nuts to the Waldens' spaniel. When Lee saw me doing this, he unexpectedly flared up. "Why would you do that? Don't you know that it could kill her?" He proceeded, much to my bewilderment, to storm into the house, taking the spaniel with him. Jillian apologized. "Don't mind Lee. He's very protective of that dog."

I remembered wistfully that my father had always disliked animals, particularly dogs; that the only pets I had ever been allowed were lone canaries and gloomy Japanese fighting fish, which sat like wilted flowers in their tanks and died within days. Twenty minutes later, Lee emerged from the house in perfect spirits, telling us that the paella was almost done and that Josephine had just called to say that she was passing the regional park and would be with us shortly. He resumed his place between my mother and Jillian, topped up his wine, and took a handful of nuts from the bowl on the table.

It was a little after eight when the daughter of the house arrived. She had her father's teeth and height, her mother's neck and hair. She was hand-in-hand with a short, scruffy creature, who I took to be her college boyfriend. After greeting everyone at the table, myself included, she settled into the seat beside me, accepted some wine, and remarked upon the pleasant aromas coming from the kitchen. Jillian took this as a cue to rise from her chair and, despite many polite protestations, was promptly followed into the house by my mother.

Over dinner, Lee began a tedious, heated discussion with Josephine's beau about politics. On either side of Mr. Walden, the older women sipped at their wine, picked at their paella, and affected to listen—eyes glazed and chins resting on their hands. Josephine, a twenty-year-old Spanish major, turned to me and asked how I was liking her old boarding school. I told her that I liked it well enough and took the opportunity to engage her in reminiscences of the S.C.C.S. faculty.

She recalled, with fondness, her former Spanish master, Señor Rafael; hulking Mr. Higginbottom, and Albert Wolfstein, whose class on modern literature she had taken as a senior. "Did you ever have Mr. Steadman?" I questioned, making every effort to control my features. "Steadman . . ." she thought for a moment; that divine name meant nothing to her. "What does he look like?"

"Oh, you know . . ." I felt my face burning. "Sort of tall. Fortyish. Dark hair. Handsome, for a teacher."

"I don't think so . . . Actually, hold on. I might've had him as a sophomore. Is he kind of touchy-feely?"

My blush deepened. "In what way?"

"Leaning a bit too close. Crouching next to your desk. That sort of thing."

"I like Mr. Steadman. He's a good teacher." Every part of me was blazing as I said this.

My mother, who I hadn't realized was listening in—having given up the pretense of caring about the men's conversation—languorously inquired. "Steadman? Isn't that the name of the friend you stayed with?"

"*Stratton*," I hissed, "Her name was Catherine Stratton."

I took a gulp of wine and, swallowing my venom, asked Josephine whether she'd heard the rumor that Mr. Wolfstein was a homosexual.

LATER THAT night, when the adults were sufficiently intoxicated and Josephine sufficiently entwined with her young man not to notice my absence, I rose from the table to make a call to Mr. Steadman. His phone rang on, without regard to my feelings. Hearing the adults' voices rising from the garden, it occurred to me that he was probably at a dinner party of his own; that I was alone and not in full possession of my faculties. I retired to the guest bedroom early to spare myself the indignity of sitting out on the patio with the rest of them, and of being awake when my mother stumbled into her nightclothes and passed out beside me, well after midnight.

She had been impressed with Arcady, as had I—insofar as I could be impressed by anything that didn't directly relate to Steadman. Early in the week, we returned to the cottage once again, and I was allowed to bathe in the green waters as my mother and the Waldens strolled about the property. "How pretty the wisteria is!" I heard my mother exclaim, entering the garden. "You should do a painting of it, Lizzie," kind Jillian remarked. Her husband, the sleaze, noticed me in the pool, pale and thin and insipid in my faded bikini. "Why don't *you* take a dip, Lizzie?" My mother tittered appreciatively.

It was agreed that Lee should contact the owners of the cottage as soon as possible. He conducted a long discussion with them late that night, with my mother hanging off his shoulder, bartering through him, to reach a tentative agreement that made her squeal and Lee dip into the cellar for a celebratory bottle.

The week, from then on, was an endless string of diversions: dinners, cafes, galleries, bookshops, and boutiques. I could see that my mother was enjoying herself and, in a detached way, hoped that she would continue doing so, even as I moped and mourned over the impropriety of the situation, the absence of Steadman, and the rapidity with which both she and I seemed to have forgotten all that had once been true. I yearned for my father as I hadn't in months, at the same time as I yearned for Steadman: confusing their images in a wholesale desire for god and man, a rejection of her and me.

Lying in the dark, clutching at phantoms, her presence at my side was loathsome. Also loathsome were the times when she changed out of one set of dark clothing and into another, shyly keeping to the opposite side of the room, as if sensing something of my aversion. As much as I tried not to look her way, some ancient lust or envy would cause my eyes to stray to her side of the room and notice various morbid details: the slight puckering of cellulite on the backs of her pale thighs; the persistent sacral dimples; her underwear, which was as lacy as anything that she had worn when I was a child, though as black as the rest of her mourning.

She was aging. She was past her prime. She would never be able to reclaim the milk and fire, the Birth-of-Venus brilliancy of her days as my father's wife. And yet, she wasn't so aged that her body had ceased to work to a monthly schedule. Indeed, as females who'd lived together for many years, we were fatefully synchronized, in that sense. This was what brought her scrambling through my toiletries bag on the morning of February the twenty-eighth, our last full day in Carmel; the bag where I happened to keep, among other things, my birth control pills.

I entered from the lounge to find her standing over my luggage with the dial of pills in her hand. I stopped dead in my tracks. She glanced up at me, flushed, and faltered. "I'm sorry . . . I wasn't . . . I was just looking for a tampon."

"In the left pocket," I said coolly, and turned on my heel to go.

The fallout didn't take place until later that day, when Jill and Josephine had absented the house with their spaniel. I was sitting on the patio stairs, reading a book on Pre-Raphaelite art that I had found earlier that week in one of the town's bookstores. Although I heard my mother come out with her coffee, I didn't look up—simply continued thumbing through the pictures, peering at the pale faces of Jane Burden, Lizzie Siddal, and Maria Zambaco. She stood behind me for several pages with her back against the balustrades, mutely fingering her mug. The gold of her wedding band glinted sadly on her dainty, white hand. "Laurel, darling, about those pills . . . ."

I sighed. "Are you really going to tell me off for this? You, of all people?"

"What do you mean, *me* of all people? I'm your mother."

"As if I had any choice about it," I muttered under my breath.

"What did you say?"

"Nothing."

"Honey, I think it's time for you to put your book away. I'm not mad. I just really need to know what's going on with you, why you felt you couldn't come to me with this. Oh, Laurel, you know all I want is for you to be happy . . ."

"I'd be happier not talking about this."

"Please don't shut me out, darling. You don't need to hide this from me. I've been there before. There's nothing wrong with what you're doing—it's a wonderful, natural thing! It's only the secrecy that makes it seem bad. Please." Her sea-green eyes shone. "Let me understand, Laurel."

My voice stuck in my throat. "You can't."

"Give me a chance! *Please.*" My mother squeezed my hand. "You're my only daughter. It upsets me that we're not close like Jill and Josie are. Don't you see that this can bring us together?" She looked beyond me with misted eyes. "I've never told you this before, but when you were younger, I sometimes had the feeling you were judging me, like you were sort of cold toward me. It can be different now. We're both old enough to try to understand each other better. Believe it or not, I do know what it's like to be in love . . ."

It took all my effort to respond in a low, seething voice. "It has nothing to do with love."

"What, then? Sex?"

"You don't understand." I shook my head, "It goes so much deeper than that. Whether you analyze it or not, there are some things that do run deep. Don't make me tell you those things. You're better off not knowing those things."

"For God's sake, can't we just talk like normal people? I don't understand why you have to be so obscure all the time. Tell me something real. Who is he? When did it start? Anything."

"I can't."

"Is it really so horrible for you to confide in me? Do you really hate me that much?"

"Please, just leave me alone. I want to read."

"Oh!" She sobbed, "I don't know why I bother. You *are* cold! You always have been! How any man can stand you . . ."

I pretended not to notice her words, nor her stormy exit into the house. For a long time after she'd gone, I remained staring at the page upon which my book lay open. On it was a picture of Millais's *Ophelia*, modeled by Lizzie Siddal. Although my tresses were not quite as copper as hers, and my beauty not as flat and mask-like, there was a resemblance. It occurred to me then that no matter how bad the situation was, I could be thankful for one thing: that it was Steadman's pills she'd found and not my father's.

WE WERE silent all the way through the two-hour ride back to San Francisco the following morning. For the first time ever, the distance between my mother and me was apparent to both of us: undisguised by the surface chatter that she'd been kind enough to supply in the past. Without this chatter, the starkness of our relationship was more terrible to me than I could ever have imagined. As we neared the south of the city, I found myself suggesting lamely, "Maybe we could stop in Colma and bring some flowers to Daddy's grave?" She appeared not to hear me.

That night, we withdrew to our separate rooms. I took the opportunity to telephone Steadman, who I hadn't spoken to in almost a week. I intended to confide in him about the argument with my mother. When he answered the phone, however, all that I could say was, "I need to see you."

"I need to see *you*, Daphne. This whole week has been wretched. Your lovely envelope—I keep coming in here to look at it. They hate me, I'm sure. Everybody hates me . . ."

"I love you. When?"

"Midday? I'll pick you up."

"Make it one o'clock." I bit my lip. "And park a few houses up. I'll find you."

"Oh, my nymph, I've been trying to write verse for you all week, but nothing sticks. I'm nothing but a hack, a sad old schoolteacher. I'm forty-three. How did that happen?"

"It's not that old," I reassured him.

"'. . . 'Tis time the heart should be unmoved/ since others it hath ceased to move . . .' Byron was only thirty-six when he wrote that. What I wouldn't give to be thirty-six again!"

He went on in that manner for some time, talking about worms and cankers and yellow leaves until I quite forgot my own woes, in sympathy for his mid-life crisis. I suspected this crisis had more to do with him being deprived of our tri-weekly pleasures than anything else, and would be alleviated the moment that I pressed my young body against him. In the meantime, I told him that I was green enough for the both of us; that he was my laureate; that he'd never grow old with me—all the while aware that there was no truth in this; that my soul was far from young; that I was merely perpetuating the myth that he loved so well.

I was not expected to accompany my mother the next day, when she went out to visit some faculty wives, including poor Jemima Hancock. She didn't leave the house until close to one. I stayed in bed, watching her walk to the Peugeot in a navy dress through the blinds of my upstairs window. Having little time to repair my appearance before Steadman's arrival, I met him as I was: hair unwashed, face clean of makeup, dressed in an old sweatshirt from the University of Heidelberg. My bare feet were shoved into bedroom slippers.

I tapped on the tinted window of the SUV. He opened the door and pulled me inside, so that my limbs were skewed awkwardly between him and the car seats. Kissing my lips, my neck, my hair, he told me that my disheveled state was very becoming; that I looked exactly like a truant schoolgirl, faking sick in order to spend her days inside making love. I disentangled myself. I asked him up to the townhouse—a proposition that he accepted boldly. Somewhere between the car and my front porch, I lost and retrieved a slipper.

I took him to the room with the daybed and pulled down the blinds. There, he had me vigorously: too vigorously, perhaps, for I felt quite bruised inside by the end of it—though, God knows, my moans had done nothing to discourage him. Afterward, he pulled up his trousers and lay back, reaching into his pocket for a pack of Dunhills. I'd told him a few weeks ago that I wouldn't mind him smoking, as long he smoked Dunhills.

I pulled on my sweatshirt, stretching it over my naked knees and drawing them to my chest. I watched him light his cigarette. I looked and felt younger than my years.

"I want to ask for a divorce," he told me inevitably, smoke curling at his fingertips.

At that, I began to cry.

WE WERE both glad to be back where we belonged on Monday. Though we had no lesson together that day, we met after school in the classroom for a coupling on his desk. He had promised, after witnessing my reaction the previous week, not to do anything rash; to in fact stay silent on the subject of divorce altogether. I couldn't help feeling, however, that he was merely humoring me; that the matter was already settled, in his mind; that he regarded my tears as little more than a feminine outburst, brought about by weakness of the nerves and a youthful incapacity to cope with big decisions; that he'd already decided what was best for me.

If my best interests did not coincide with his children's, he didn't admit it. Instead, he rationalized his poor parenting. "Cathy and Cole don't need me. They're not little kids anymore," or "You should see the deadly looks that my daughter gives me, these days. She doesn't want me around."

I thought that I knew the source of these deadly looks. Way back in December, after taking me to that awful clinic and subsequently parking for half an hour in a dark grove of oaks, Steadman had dropped me off in his SUV at the field-side parking lot. It was a windswept day. A few younger girls were standing about on the playing field in bright red soccer jerseys, arms akimbo. Stepping out of my gas-guzzling steed, I caught sight of another gleam of red among the shrubbery. It eventually metamorphosed into the thin, jerseyed back of Karen Harmsworth's sister, bent over the errant ball. I slammed the car door. My Mary Janes crunched over the gravel. The freshman straightened up, ball under arm, and peered at me with her pale, husky-dog eyes. We both flinched as Steadman backed out of the parking lot with an indelicate honk of his horn.

From that day on, whenever I saw Karen Harmsworth's little sister in hallways and bathroom queues, I felt her eyes on me. Sometimes, if she were with a crowd of other freshmen, they would all look at me. Karen herself, who I had the mis-fortune of having in my English class, would sometimes cast a stolid, curious eye my way, especially when Steadman was near my desk. Thankfully, her glances had none of the insistence of her younger sister's.

I tried to take the issue up with Steadman one day, when he was complaining of his children's diminished respect for him. "Doesn't your daughter have a friend at this school?"

"Cathy? I don't think so."

"She had some photos in her room . . ." I paused, afraid that he might not have approved of my trespass. He remained unfazed. ". . . with Karen Harmsworth's little sister."

"Which one is that?"

"Small. Freckles. Short, black hair. Creepy eyes."

"Ah." Steadman laughed. "I think I've seen that one. Not much to look at, is she?"

"That's not the point. I'm worried she might know something. I've seen her staring at me."

He laughed again. "I wouldn't worry about her. She's a queer one. She probably just likes the look of you."

"I don't think so. What if she's told Cathy?"

"So be it. The kids are going to have to find out eventually. After all . . ." This was a tasteless joke of his, "You might be their stepmother, someday."

It irked me that he could take it all so lightly when, for me, our situation was nothing if not dire. Like poor Heloise, I was fated to find more sweetness in the word "whore" than "wife." I saw myself as Steadman's whore, his fetish, his poetic indiscretion—nothing more permanent than that. At the hint of anything more permanent, my head instantly became crowded with counterarguments; considerations of age, family, and temperament that made our love seem ill-starred, instead of the miracle of cosmic alignment that it really was. For, whenever I cast my mind back, all the way back, to that initial meeting, I couldn't help being struck by how divinely arranged it had been. Every detail, from the dead father to the trees I sat under, to the whiteness of his shirt, had conspired to bring us together.

I was afraid of straying too far from the poetry of this initial connection. Though I was still his nymph, though he still showered me with poetry, he did little to protect me from the realities that hurtled toward me like a bulldozer through woods. In fact, more often than not, he was that bulldozer—trampling the greenness that he, as much as I, needed to uphold. It wasn't only the references he made to our future, to us living together as man and teen wife: it was the sloppiness, the ignorance of aesthetic truth, that such references implied.

I had fallen in love with his contradictions, with his blend of flesh and godliness, bourgeois and bohemian, brute lust and cold refinement. This love hadn't changed. My ability to cope with it, however, had. In the years before Steadman, when I was still my father's daughter, I had hated contradiction; had, in fact, been willing to break the incest taboo to avoid it. Somewhere, deep inside, this girl still existed. This girl was suffocating under the strain of her own principles. This girl was gasping for God.

It was difficult for me to think of my father then, for more reasons than I cared to name. I knew that, in life, he'd been an insignificant man—little more than a luckless wraith, who had experienced a decade of bliss in my mother's earthly garden, only to return to his abject natural state. I knew that I was partly responsible for this abjection; that I'd never loved him as I should have; that my current attachment to his memory was shadowy at best, and had more to do with his instrumentality in uniting me with Steadman than any special qualities of his mind. For all this, I clung to the idea of his divinity: a divinity that was utterly impotent and could do nothing for me in life, but that comforted me with its sweet, cold, sad finality.

It was a divinity that had nothing to do with that of my Apollo. In him, a deeply dependent and almost repulsively physical nature had been paired with something inhuman—an underlying, cold-blooded aversion to anything on the side of life. It was this aversion, I suspected, that led him to choose me as a mistress and not a girl better suited to the fulfilment of lust: a lively girl, a womanly girl, a girl without neuroses, a girl utterly devoid of poetry.

He did not like women. As I was not a woman, but rather, a Waterhouse nymph (tall, lithe, lovely, doomed, nubile, pale as frost, with small schoolgirl breasts tipped with pink, and a broad, bony pelvis), this need not have bothered me then. Someday, however, if I were to go on living, I would be forced to become a woman; to take on the essential characteristics that disgusted me as much as they did him. It was my misfortune to have been born into a sex that I despised, a sex whose inherent physicality precluded all hopes of divinity. I would not allow myself to lapse into womanhood without a fight. I would sooner die than become the thing I hated, the thing that bred hatred.

I couldn't go on pretending that he was only his lust, or that the continued service of his lust was what he really wanted. When he took possession of me, I saw beyond the hot blood to the cold desire to shape, fix, and stifle all that was alive in me. His desire was to possess me and, through possession, to take more of my life away. I would let myself be taken until I was nothing more than his creation, a poetic body, the divine alternative to womankind.

THAT WE'D passed a whole season cloistered together in his classroom, away from the elements of our bitter California winter, was difficult to believe. Although rains continued through most of March and the mornings remained cold enough to merit a sweater, I could sense a change in the air. I began to notice my classmates sporting socks in place of stockings and shedding their gray knitwear whenever they chanced upon a patch of sunlight or felt a room to be particularly overheated. The freshmen had begun to look like sophomores, the sophomores like juniors, the juniors like seniors, and the seniors, somewhat to my malaise, like college girls.

Even the content of our lessons had changed, becoming looser, more open to interpretation, and requiring a heightened level of individual thought and inquiry. Having handed in our essays on Blake's *America*, we were done with the British Romantic poets and given a neat segue into the next component of the course: the American Romantics. For this segment, we were to read critical works by Emerson, selections from Thoreau's *Walden*, and later, when it was warm enough for us to return outside for Fridays, the poetry of Whitman, Dickinson, and Poe.

I ignored the general buzz among my year group about college acceptances, most of which were due during Holy Week. As others jittered and stressed, I privately fretted, less afraid of rejection than I was of its unlikelihood. I yearned for some stupefying miracle to put a halt to my progress and so preserve me in his classroom, in his arms, for all time. Alas, I was too much of a coward to let myself flunk completely, attending Slawinski's Tuesday afternoon sessions until I regained my B average and practicing my French accent to Madame Rampling's content. One day, sitting in my lover's lap, I gave voice to my misgivings, nuzzling against him and sulking. "I don't want to go to college. I really don't. Please, can't you just teach me forever?"

He laughed. "You overestimate me, my child. In a year, you'll have surpassed me. No doubt, you'll have all the professors chasing after you . . ."

"I don't want professors. I want this."

"This?"

"Poetry," I elaborated, "And art. And love. And I want you to teach me Italian. I'm sick of learning French."

"Well, I'd be more than willing to supplement you, in those departments. When we marry, we'll have all our evenings together. I daresay you'll be bored to death of poetry . . ."

Glumly, I wondered whether he would be bored of me, by that point. I toyed with his tie and inquired coyly, "I'm not bored of poetry, but do we really have to read *Walden?*"

"You don't like Thoreau? What a pity. I was going to see if you wanted to make an excursion with me this weekend to the woods. Purely educational, of course. We'd be examining the plant life, discoursing on the transcendental effects of nature on the human soul. You'd be bored out of your mind, I expect . . ."

Throughout the spring, he was to abduct me several times from the campus, with the intention of driving me out to this or that hiking trail, state park, or preserve. Thankfully, my status as a senior, set to graduate in a matter of months, gave me some leeway when it came to signing out for unchaperoned activities. More than once, I even forged a letter from my mother, insisting that Laurel Eloise Marks be permitted to leave the school grounds for the better part of a Saturday, to make the pilgrimage to her dear father's gravesite. I was amazed by how few eyebrows were raised by this request. At the appointed time, my lover would pick me up in his dark-windowed vehicle from one of the less-frequented gates of the girls' school, and from there we would make off toward hills and valleys, swimming in fog or crested with redwoods, as well as convenient thickets of artemisia, bay, and bracken.

For obvious reasons, we preferred foggy days to clear ones, thickly wooded areas to sparse hillocks, and dubious, dirt trails to those that were more frequently trodden. He took me off the tracks and, against tree trunks or in the undergrowth, would clutch and force and bite, with barely a semblance of gentleness. Sometimes, the cracking of a twig or the crunching of gravel would cause him to break away, just as he was on the point of possessing me, and—sullen, engorged, adjusting himself—to march me to the privacy of his parked vehicle. Other times, too far gone for that, he'd simply clutch me tighter, force himself into me further, and bite into the skin of my neck, covering my mouth with his hand in an attempt to stifle my fine, mist-like sighs.

At least once, we hazarded to meet on a day when it was raining heavily, and confined ourselves to his SUV. He parked off the road, not far from school. He had told his wife that he was going out for gardening supplies and, in fact, really did need to buy some. This he explained to me while fumbling in the glove compartment for his Dunhills, after an awkward entanglement in the backseat, which we both emerged from

with bruises. I laughed bitterly. I thought of his hothouse.
I thought of his suburban bungalow and his slim, lenient,
pediatrician wife. I thought of his pouting son and his plump
daughter, who didn't resemble me in the least, and for whom
he had no improper feelings. I thought that any man would be
crazy to give this all up for a whore of seventeen, with bruises
on her limbs and a buried father, beneath a flowerless head-
stone in Colma.

On Lazarus Saturday, the last day of March, I was obliged to
return to my mother once more for the Easter holidays. In the
weeks since I'd seen her last, our contact had been minimal: she
phoned only twice—the second time, on March the thirtieth,
to confirm that she was picking me up the next morning—and
wrote only one brief letter, informing me that she had put the
townhouse on the market and found a buyer for my father's
Lexus. All the same, it seemed that she was willing to recover
something of our former, superficial relations. I mentioned that
I was in need of a gown to wear to the end-of-year dance at
Trinity Catholic College. An obliging parent, she offered to
take me shopping the following Saturday.

After a mere six months, she had traded her black clothes
for half mourning, a development that coincided mysteriously with the revelation of my non-virginity. Throughout
Holy Week—the only time of the year, aside from Christmas,
that my family had ever been rigorous with churchgoing—we
attended services at St. Dominic's, with the widow looking
lukewarm in shades of gray, dark blue, and lavender. Steadman,
as he confided in me over the phone one evening, was exempt
from attending the Presbyterian church that his wife and children frequented; had always been exempt, having refused,

years ago, to trade in the Catholicism that he had been raised with and later abandoned for her watered down WASPism. Long before we met, he had considered himself, in his pseudo-Byronic manner, to be something of a lost soul, a restless non-believer—and yet, it was apparent to me that he still retained that original sense of guilt, sin, and hell; that he still yearned for judgment; that he yearned to feel himself accused by some higher power, divine or otherwise.

I listened patiently as he told me about his break from the church during his late teens; about his defiance of his mother, who had become increasingly fat and overbearing; of how he effectively became like his father, studying medicine and bedding a lot of women until he finally met Danielle. When asked what was different about her, he told me simply that she was "good"; that she was unlike any of the others; that she had made him want to be a better person—though, obviously, not enough to keep his hands off me.

During our bedtime conversations, I stayed silent about the letters that had begun to show up on my doorstep, morning after morning. With every acceptance, I became further embedded in my own indecision. I had not felt so powerless, so drained of will and the ability to think for myself, since the weekend that he had driven me back to boarding school after I bled on his wife's sheets. The only decision that I was capable of making was that I was incapable of deciding; that I had to defer to my master, to have him settle the matter for me.

We had arranged a tryst for Thursday afternoon, a time when I knew that my mother would be busy with the realtor. He picked me up and drove us a few blocks away from my house, stopping to search through the road map that he would come to rely on so much, when selecting locations for our *plein air* amours. "We could go to Camino Alto . . . that's eleven miles . . . Cascade Canyon . . . that's twenty miles . . . I did say I would be back for dinner, though . . ."

I sighed. I took out the acceptance letters that I had folded away inside my handbag, and imitated him. "I could go to St. Mary's . . . that's forty-five minutes from you . . . Pomona or Claremont McKenna . . . they're both better schools, but seven hours away . . . Gettysburg . . . that's across the country, you know, I'll need a plane to get to you . . . Bryn Mawr . . . they've offered me a scholarship . . ."

My voice cracked. Against my will, I began to cry.

"Darling!" he put his arms around me and secreted away the letters, reading them behind my back, "But this is wonderful, darling! It'll be a new life for both of us. *Incipit vita nova.* And that scholarship could come in handy. I'm afraid we won't be rolling in cash, once the divorce is finalized."

"You want me to go to Bryn Mawr?" I asked, looking up at him.

"Well, it's your decision, of course. It does have the inestimable advantage of being a ladies' college, though, meaning I'll have fewer rivals to worry about." He said this with one of his charming, sharp-canined smiles. "Besides, I think we've both been in California for too long. Don't you want to go somewhere different? Somewhere far from your friends and your mother and everything else that might come between us?"

"Where will you work?"

"My child, Philadelphia has the largest Catholic-school system in the country. I'm sure I'll find another job teaching." He stroked my hair and gave me an indulgent glance, "At an all-boys school, of course."

It was too much. Yet again, I broke into tears.

"Laurel, Laurel, Laurel . . ." he murmured, taking me in his arms, "don't despair. We'll have a nice life. I'll teach boys during the day, and at night, I'll come home to you. We can marry. We'll be together, we will!"

"Are you really going to divorce her?" What I meant to ask was *Do you really have to divorce her?*

"I've been saying that for weeks, haven't I? Trust me, darling, this is only the beginning. We'll be free, soon enough. Won't it be wonderful not to have to sneak around anymore? To have a place of our own? A bed? Oh, my Daphne . . ." He caressed me furiously, "Let's get a room somewhere now. Shall we? Shall we?"

I COULD not find the words to express to him the idiocy of a grown man divorcing his wife of sixteen years for the sake of young flesh: flesh that had already been his, countless times, yet that he felt the need to ascribe permanency to; to make his own before the eyes of God, the government, and all the other invisible jurors who he'd defied by touching me in the first place. I could not, did not want to find the words, and so went along with all that he had told me, sparing hardly a thought for its idiocy.

My mother was already home by the time that I returned, barelegged and befouled, from the motel that he had taken me to, and where he had taken pains to pleasure me, as if believing that a single, bodily shudder would be enough to cure me of my existential woes. She looked at me critically when I came in, putting aside her book. "Are you going to bathe before church?" I nodded and tramped upstairs, taking the smell of my sins with me.

On Easter Saturday, the two of us drove into the city as planned for a day of shopping at Union Square. In department-store dressing rooms, I tried on gown after gown, before settling on a floaty number in green chiffon. It had a high neckline, though left most of my back quite bare, emphasizing the fragile sharpness of my shoulder blades, the incurve of my young spine; I had shed those three pounds, and some. Without batting an eyelash, my mother put the purchase on her credit card and told me that I would need a bag and shoes to go with it. I wondered whether she was hoping to buy my confidence; to inspire me to tell her about my "nice boy" by helping me be more desirable to him.

I had informed Steadman in passing of my plans for that afternoon. He paid me an unexpected phone call while I was strapping on some stilettos at Neiman Marcus, half an hour later. "Where are you?" His voice was hushed, excited.

"NM's, women's accessories. Why?"

"No reason. What are you doing?"

"Looking at shoes." I saw that my mother was approaching. "Listen, I have to go. Can we talk later?"

"Of course, my love," he said smoothly and dialed off.

"How are those?" my mother asked of the high heels, standing before me with her purse in hand.

"Too tight. I think I need the nine and a half."

"What did I tell you?" She allowed herself a smug tap of her own size sevens.

We had just paid for the shoes and were strolling toward the handbag section, when I caught sight of a lone, male shopper, out of place in the gynocentric surroundings. I felt a thrill of humiliation and arousal. I wondered whether it would be possible to pass him by without my mother seeing him. With the instincts of a stalker, perfectly attuned to his prey, however, my lover turned from the display of handbags that he had been pretending to inspect and dazzled us both with a charmingly uneven smile. He was wearing his chino pants and a cheerful, check shirt that was reserved for weekends. "Laurel! Mrs. Marks! What a pleasant surprise."

I felt my mother stiffen beside me. It seemed that she had become less receptive to strangers, in the last few months. He continued, oblivious to her frigidity.

"Perhaps you don't remember me. I'm Catherine's father. Laurel stayed with us over Thanksgiving."

"I remember," my mother responded coolly.

"Your daughter really is a delight!" He placed a firm hand on my shoulder—a bold move, even for him. "We would love to have her again sometime. In fact, what about tonight? I'm sure Catherine would be thrilled . . ."

"I don't think that would be appropriate. We have plans as a family tomorrow for Easter. Besides," she narrowed her pale eyes at him, "it's about time we had *your* daughter come to stay. I've been dying to meet her."

"Oh, no, Mom," I was quick to object. "We can't have people over. The house is a mess."

This was true enough. Since settling on a price for Arcady, my mother had been busy sorting through the contents of the townhouse, deciding the fate of each item. Mr. Steadman concealed his disappointment with a strained smile. "That's a pity. Maybe in the summer . . . Laurel, don't be a stranger . . . Mrs. Marks . . ." He offered her his hand.

"Mr. Stratton, isn't it?" my mother posed, accepting the handshake.

"Steadman," he corrected her, not understanding the cautionary glance that I shot him. "Hugh Steadman."

As soon as my suitor had skulked away, I sought to change the subject, drawing my mother's attention to the beading on a nearby evening bag. It was some time before I was able to calm the thudding of my heart, the fluttering of my nerves. At the checkout, forking out for the final purchase of the day, my mother complained of a headache and suggested that we take afternoon tea at the Rotunda before making the drive home. When I was younger, she had often treated me to tea there after a long day of shopping, and this memory made me sick at heart. I agreed, tensely; if she were going to confront me about what she had seen, I supposed that it would be safer if she did so in public.

We ascended to the fourth floor and were seated at a table for two overlooking the lobby, beneath the golden, stained-glass dome ceiling. I pursed my lips as a starched serviette was spread out over my lap. My mother ordered for the both of us. There was a chill, water-sipping silence. In my handbag, my cell phone began to buzz. Our eyes locked. I excused myself.

I pushed my way out of the restaurant. He wanted me to meet him in the lobby. I told him that I could not. He persisted, arguing that it would only take a few minutes. I was weak and seeking any excuse to escape her; I took the next elevator down. I spied him among the smattering of people on the ground floor and, my heavy Mary Janes clip-clopping, hastened to meet him. I was white-socked and pinafore-dressed. He was check-shirted and carrying a shiny new shopping bag. I thought it best not to embrace him.

"I bought you something," he said a little sheepishly.

"How nice."

"Here." He extended the shopping bag toward me. "Take it."

I didn't doubt that it was lingerie, and felt almost as embarrassed for him as I did for myself. I accepted the bag. Without inspecting its contents, I sequestered it inside my purse. "Thank you."

Having smiled and curtsied, I was about to turn on my heel and go. "Wait!" He caught my arm. Undoing all my discretion, he pulled me close to him and ensnared me in a deep, long, roving kiss, right there in the department-store lobby. When, at last, he loosed his hold, I wiped my lips and backed away, nodding a speechless farewell. I crossed back to the elevator, hot-faced and down-headed and, only when I was inside, looked into the bag that he had given me. I saw sheer fabric and lace edging, as expected. I touched my burning lips.

In my absence, the tea and tiered-cake stand had been set down. My hands trembled as I retrieved my serviette from the table and smoothed it over my lap. "I waited for you before starting." My mother's voice was strained and thin. "Thank you. It looks very good," I said of the scones, sandwiches, and *petits fours*. As she poured her tea and milk and spooned sugar into the rust-colored mixture, I saw that her hands were trembling even more furiously than my own.

HAD SHE asked me, I would have confessed to everything that night. As it was, the woman had been stunned into silence and didn't dare to accuse me, either over our barely touched afternoon tea or in the northbound traffic home. Even the most venomous word, I felt, would have been better than that silence, in which I saw my shadowy deeds looming, assuming uglier forms. The man between the daughter's thighs wore checks and chino pants. The man was old enough to be her father. What could this knowledge mean to the widow behind the wheel, shading her eyes against the late sun?

Passing her bedroom door that evening on my way back from the bathroom, I thought that I heard sobbing. The Caravaggio was still in the hall: prim young Judith beheading the bearded chief. I couldn't bring myself to breach that threshold, to enter the room where it had all begun. I locked myself in my own chamber and wept into my stale pillowcase.

"I suppose I won't see you until your graduation." This was the last thing that my mother said to me, dropping me off at school on Tuesday. She presented me her cool cheek to brush and I got a whiff of her perfume: first love, fragrance on throat.

There were no classes that day. Steadman met me in his SUV and we made love among the live oak and madrone.

I KNEW in my heart that there was nothing left for us to do but separate before any more damage was done. I knew this, yet I was prevented from doing anything about it because I was weak, greedy, sensuous; because I couldn't stand to go without the sins that he had accustomed me to until all the pleasure I reaped from them ran dry. His love was the only stimulus that I was capable of responding to, any longer. I sought it out as frequently and forcefully as I could get it.

A carelessness had come over us with the sense of how little time we had left. He had handed in his letter of resignation, effective mid-June. With this, he considered himself released from his teacherly duties in all but the official sense. As an instructor, he showed none of the inspiration, the enthusiasm for his work that he had when we fell in love. He was often grim. His mind wandered. He checked his brown-and-gold wristwatch and glanced outside the window, thrumming his fingers on the desk. He eyed my lips, my throat, my legs.

When we resumed our Friday lessons outdoors, I took my rightful place by his side in the shade of the willows, looking over his shoulder as he droned on and the minds of my coevals strayed. Afterward, I would help him carry the books upstairs, in defiance of the looks that were cast our way. Better still, I would wander off to our laurel arbor to await him in a vain attempt to relive the loss of my virginity.

It was April then and my world was shrinking, flourishing with spring green and flowers of hysteria. I had read somewhere that suicides multiply during fine weather and this made sense to me: whereas fall had sympathized with my melancholy, spring made a mockery of it. Only the truly forlorn could have seen the ugliness of birds in rape-flight, of wasps haunting the school trashcans, and the excruciating paleness of newly shaved legs. Only the truly forlorn could have smelled all the death in the air.

I chased the smell of death. I was careless. I took to meeting him every day after school, and Saturdays, too, whenever we could both get away from our respective jailers. One afternoon, waiting for him in his empty classroom, I didn't even bother to close the door completely, but sat on his desk swinging my legs, for anyone to see. People did see, not the least of whom was Mrs. Faherty, whose lynx eye remarked me from behind gold-rimmed glasses. She strode into the doorway, hands on hip replacement. "Excuse me! What do you think you're doing in there?"

"I'm just . . . waiting for Mr. Steadman. He said that I could see him about my English essay."

"Well, wait outside!" She shooed me out of the room. "Really, it's unthinkable for you to be here after school hours. This is private property!"

I had never seen Mrs. Faherty so close up and was surprised by how oddly straight and white her teeth were. I wondered if they were false. With an effort, I looked her in the face. "I'm sorry. He told me his door would be open . . ."

"What is your name?"

"Laurel Marks."

"Go wait on that bench, Laurel Marks. I don't care what he told you. These are the rules. If I see you in here again . . ."

She went on and on and I nodded duteously, my eyes glazed with boredom and contempt. The hag was still lecturing me from some paces away when Steadman arrived, finding me sitting disconsolately with my chin in hand, watching my fellow students walk by. "Laurel! Sorry to keep you waiting, my dear . . ." He nodded dismissively at Mrs. Faherty. "Dierdre, good afternoon."

"I was just telling this one how unacceptable, how truly unacceptable, it is for her to be loitering inside empty class-rooms . . ."

"Nonsense. There's no reason for her to have to wait in the crowded hallway," my lover replied smoothly, then, with admirable male insensitivity, turned his attentions back to me. "Come inside, Laurel. Dierdre, will you excuse us? I can take it from here."

He closed the door behind us and, after contenting himself that she had moved along, set the lock. I sat back down on his desk and recrossed my legs. He clucked his tongue humorously. "Loitering in empty classrooms, Laurel? How *truly* unacceptable."

We were reckless enough to take such close shaves in our stride, to remain stolid in the face of the schoolgirl gossip that I was almost certain we were a subject of. While waiting around outside French class one morning, I overheard Amanda remark to Marcelle, "Seamus is an idiot. I need someone more mature." She looked askance at me and lowered her voice, "Of course, not as mature as *you-know-who*."

"Who?" I inquired, regardless of the fact that I was not part of their conversation.

"Never mind," they chorused, eyeing me sharply.

The end was in sight for both of us, though we couldn't have perceived it more differently. Since the beginning of the year, he'd lost a whole two inches from his waistline, as a result of taking up smoking and skipping so many lunches to have it off with me. He purchased new trousers in black, brown, and olive green to fit his slimmed-down waist. He purchased some very smart striped shirts, and a new pair of black wingtips. As far as he was concerned, he was in the prime of his life, unaware of the fact that the young body that he wielded was nothing more than a glorified carcass, beautiful carrion.

Whether indoors or outdoors, I gave myself up to the torments of our love, which left me shaking, hot and cold as one afflicted by fever. With increasing frequency, I cried after our couplings, causing my Apollo to take me in his arms, to coax and plead and repent. When all else failed, he'd simply grit his teeth and drive me back to campus, dropping me off somewhere outside the main gates.

THERE WAS a part of me that yearned to put him off, to sicken him with my instability, and so drive him back into the stable arms of his wife of sixteen years. There was a part of me that wanted to remind him that we had nothing of that staying power, that sixteen months together would've been a stretch for us. There was a part of me that wanted him to know that the future he piled before me was too rich to be palatable, like dessert on an anorexic's plate. There was a part of me that wanted to flaunt its own insanity, to send him running from my rotting, dark woods and back home to his bungalow.

He had no obligation to marry me. I was not some nineteenth-century virgin who, robbed of her hymen, had lost her market value. What motivated him to stay with me, through my crying jags and sulks, was not honor but the stubbornness of his own desire for me. It was plain to see that I was still desirable to him, for all my mental frailty; that this frailty, if anything, made me more desirable.

Everywhere, the phantom of his manhood pursued me. I began to feel him in me, even when we were separated by a span of hours; felt him shaking me, bruising me, soothing me with hot sap. My loins were constantly tingling. My movements and belladonna-black pupils betrayed to the whole world the perversion of my mind. From a limpid nymph, I had developed into something far less poetic: a nymphomaniac.

Though no substitute for the English Romantics, whose words had been my first seduction, my hidden flower and winter withering, I was inspired by the singsong sadomasochism of

Emily Dickinson, who never had a Steadman of her own. Likewise, I couldn't hear my lover reciting Poe without thinking back to what he had told us about the poet's usage of the letter L, the loveliest letter in the English language, and the poet's insistence that there could be no topic more worthy of literature than the death of a beautiful woman.

I was haunted by what I knew to be true: that there was no truth, other than beauty. With the passage of each day and the dwindling of each week in carnal acts whose exact details were becoming ever more forgettable, I felt the truth chilling my blood and turning my thoughts in the direction that poetic justice had always intended them to turn. "Tell me again about the wood of suicides," I sighed to him softly, while we were lying in the undergrowth one afternoon, at the height of spring. He obliged me.

"Dante and Virgil enter the wood. There is no path. The trees are rotten and deformed. Their leaves are black and drip with venomous, dark blood. Hideous, bloated harpies tear at the leaves, making their nests in the branches. All through the wood, the moaning of the souls encased in bark can be heard. Dante plucks a leaf from one of the trees, causing the soul within to wail and bleed. The poor, damned soul is a virtuous suicide, a jurist who killed himself after he was imprisoned under false pretenses. He attributes his downfall to *La Meretrice* . . ."

"The whore."

"Not just any whore. Envy."

Had he never come to me that day in the woods back in November, it is possible that he might have loved me forever; might have mourned forever the passage of my chaste beauty, and devoted the rest of his life to immortalizing it in verse. As it was, I could never have been satisfied with mere love: I had to be *known*, and everything this implied—every parting of the legs, every raising of the kilt, every palpating digit, stimulating me to the point of madness. I needed to be known, and so had condemned us both to a rut of lust and gratification, which there was only one foreseeable way of getting out of.

Speaking of what was to become of us after I graduated, we both realized that nothing definitive could be done in terms of cohabitation and the transportation across state borders while I was still legally a minor. Having rather miraculously avoided detection for the seven months that he had known me, unlawfully, it would have been folly to risk everything by taking me from under my mother's nose at the age of seventeen years and ten months. I would be eighteen in mid-August. On August 12, 2003, I would effectively be an adult; effectively be capable of running away with, sleeping with, even marrying a man twenty-five years my senior, without breaking any laws. All that was required were two months of abstinence, in which to sort out our affairs and await the legalization of my young body. Two months for him to forget all that he knew.

He would sort out his affairs. He would do his utmost to find lodgings in the Philadelphia Main Line, to find himself a teaching post somewhere nearby. Meanwhile, I would age and wait, dreading the day that he would come for me and take me away from the last shreds of my greenness, into the black, decaying mass of adulthood. He would come for me. He would take me out of Arcadia and drive me all the way from Monterey County, CA, to Pennsylvania—meandering through the deserts and mountains of the middle states, staying overnight in motor courts and chalets, to arrive at Bryn Mawr in time for the start of fall semester. Or such was the plan. He told me he'd be divorced by then and that we could marry along the way, in the state of my choice. I told him that he should wait until we'd settled in before so much as filing for a divorce from Mrs. Danielle Steadman. My lover needed all the time that I could buy him.

As we approached nearer and nearer to the date of our parting, my feverishness was paired with an unexpected coolness of mind, which didn't at all proceed from rationality. That I no longer cried after making love was something he could only interpret positively, perceiving nothing of the fatal resolve that it indicated. I had ceased to care for myself almost entirely and, by extension, cared less for my beloved Steadman. I was distancing myself further every day, even as I continued to desire him, to profess my undying devotion.

I was both terrified and relieved to think that my love for him was coming to an end; that the starvation of my sexuality over the summer would be enough to turn me off the man and pledge me forever to the other, the god. For a time, god and man had been inseparable. I had come to see, however, that, in the long run, they were incompatible, just as divinity and womanhood were incompatible, or art and life. I loved him, in those last weeks, with a love that knew its own perishability, a love that threw up its arms and rejoiced in the leaf-shadings, the all-pervading odor of dark earth and chlorine. In the car, in the classroom, in the copses, I loved him enough to feel that—without freeing myself from the whirlwind of lust—his knowledge of me was absolute; that we had loved enough to justify an eternity of torment.

We ran out of coursework early in the summer. Most lessons of his had come to be conducted outdoors, by the glittering lake that separated Saint Cecilia's from Trinity, where the seniors' dance was to be held on the last Friday of term. I was the near-naked girl of greener days. I spoke with him softly beneath the whispering willows, after the rest of the class had been given permission to engage in private reading, conversation, sunbathing, and just about anything else that would keep them occupied while he courted me. Nobody cared about our dissolution. The atmosphere was one of such license, such sun-soaked bliss, that he could even be observed to briefly rest his hand on mine or whisper in my ear.

It was not only our English lessons that gave out under the influence of the season. In art class, Ms. Faber invited us to make use of anything in the supplies closet for untutored drawing and painting. In gym, which I had altogether given up attending, Ms. Da Silva was said to have escorted the class to the aquatic center at Trinity, where they splashed and shrieked and, soaking wet, enjoyed the lewd glances of schoolboys while traversing the fields back to the girls' campus. The better part of my other lessons was spent rereading Ovid's *Metamorphoses*, an occupation that went unnoticed by my now indifferent instructors. Over and over again, I became Daphne, pursued by a panting god through the thickets of Arcadia. Over and over again, I let myself be caught, kissed, before I could so much as formulate my prayer for transformation. By the last week of the semester, I had taken to slipping out of the room whenever I had math or biology, to visit my love in the English Department. He would welcome with an embrace that confused cold wood with the warmth and softness of condemned flesh.

He conducted his final lesson outside with us on Thursday, fourth period. Before the lunch bell went, he made his parting comments to the senior class, announcing that he too wouldn't be returning to the school in September; that he wished us all the best in our future endeavors; that he felt privileged to have contributed to the education of such an upstanding group of young women. The upstanding young women yawned, scratched, and smiled placidly, unmoved by his valediction. A few exchanged snide glances.

It seemed like a lifetime ago that he'd first taken us outside, as his attendant nymphs, to listen to him reading Wordsworth and luxuriate in the last sun of September. Since then, he had lost his following. He had lost more than he cared to admit. After the lesson, I went deep into the woods with him and consoled him as best as I could. "To think," he said bitterly, smoothing his hands over the pleats of my kilt, "this is the last time I'll ever see you in your uniform."

I had vowed not to cry that day. I looped my arms around his warm neck and kissed him softly. He tasted faintly of tobacco. "But you will be there, tomorrow night?"

"I'll be there. In my best dinner jacket." His wan smile did nothing to conceal the break in his voice.

I didn't go to last period math, but stayed with him until dusk, accompanying him all the way to the staff parking lot. We were as tragic as any young lovers, who circumstances had conspired to separate. Watching his silver SUV, my would-be ride into the future, alloy with the golden sun, I broke my vow and dissolved into tears.

THERE WERE no classes on Friday. Instead, the time was set aside for packing, with many of the younger students being sent for by their parents soon after breakfast. For the girls in my grade, there were additional preparations to be made for that evening's dance and the subsequent morning's graduation ceremony. I had made an appointment at the campus salon, as much to distract myself from my inner turmoil as to ensure my own loveliness that night. In a recent staff meeting, Steadman had volunteered to play the piteous part of chaperon at the dance. That night would be our final meeting as master and pupil; our final meeting as anything, if I were to admit to myself the disease at my core, blackening my blood and slowly poisoning every cell in my young body.

"Aren't you beautiful?" The lady at the salon held a mirror to the back of my head. She had done my hair up in an elegant, low chignon, with stray curls wisping over my face.

At seven in the evening, buses dropped us off in front of Trinity. Thin-legged in my high heels and floaty green dress, I looked every bit the forest-dwelling nymph. The ballroom was amber-lit, already teeming with staff and schoolboys. Due to the comparative largeness of the boys' school, there was an obvious surplus of young men, which the organizers had compensated for by dispensing with the four-couple tables of Homecoming and seating us alphabetically, in one long conglomeration. Scott Maccoby, some seats up from me, gave me an aloof nod, and took to flirting with Rose Macpherson. I cast my eyes across the room, to the much smaller faculty table, though could see no sign of Steadman. Had he crashed his car on the way over? Had his wife forbidden him from leaving the house? Had he simply decided that he couldn't bear seeing me?

"So, where are you going for college?" the boy at my right— "Jake Marone," according to his place card—asked me from behind his acne.

"I'm not going to college." This was a convenient conversation killer.

I had shot down three more Trinity boys and given away my entrée—a single pillow of lobster ravioli—to another before my master arrived. My heart leaped into my mouth. I drained the contents of my glass and stood up, intent on the dark corner from which he scanned the room. The music had started up again and couples were slowly trickling onto the dance floor.

"Dance?" A sweaty, fat palm was held up at my left ("Gabriel Mapp"). "I owe you for that ravioli."

"Have my dinner too," I said coolly, and proceeded to cross the floor alone.

I couldn't help feeling exposed out of uniform, finding him amid the clamor of the dance hall. It occurred to me that every soul in the room was likely to outlive me: from Mitzi Gantz lurking near the punch bowl; to Marcelle in her fuchsia dress, laughing against Flynn's shoulder; to my very own love, standing with his hands in his trouser pockets. His eyes were bright in the shadows. He looked ever so handsome in his dinner jacket. I greeted him shyly, stooping my head and clutching at my skirt in a graceless half-curtsy. "You're late."

He looked at me humorlessly, noting my bare shoulders and the beauty of my upswept curls. "You're lovely."

I reached for his right hand and gave it a covert squeeze, my fingers fumbling over the coolness of his wedding band. "Do you like my dress?"

"'. . . a nameless girl in freshest summer greens . . .'" was all that he said, somewhat wistfully.

"I have a name," I countered.

"Too sacred to utter, I'm afraid."

"Say it. No one else needs to hear."

"Laurel. My Laurel."

"Hugh," I said, for what was perhaps the first time. "My Hugh."

He passed a gentle, fatherly hand up my bare arm and onto my bony shoulder. So much, perhaps, was acceptable in a dark corner. I quivered with desire and regret. I asked whether we could please, dear sir, go outside.

"Let me go first. I'll distract whoever's at the door," he replied and, just as he was about to exit, smoothed a not-so-acceptable hand over my naked back. I shivered at the touch.

I pushed my way into the crowded bathroom. I washed my hands and eyed my ghost in the mirror. Everything about me was as pale, frail, and green as it would ever be. I slipped out of the bathroom, out of the ballroom, and into the chill, early summer night.

My lover stood by the door, smoking with a grim Trinity guardsman, from somewhere in our distant past. Behind the doorkeeper's back, he caught my eye and nodded to the lure of the dark woods beyond the rowing shed. I kept to the shadows, to the sides of unknown buildings. The muffled laughter of couples, drinking and groping through the night, was a cold burst of air to my ears. He had seen me escape downhill, past the shed, willowy among the willows. I knew that he would not pursue me until I was safely concealed by my natural element, nor would I halt until we reached that hallowed ground— though it was a long way from that side of the lake to our own private arbor.

I did not slow down, even when I felt that he was behind me. My high heels stuck in the dirt and my bare, pale back was certain to make me easy to spy against the black of the tree trunks. His eager tread reached me as a rustle of leaves, growing ever closer. His breath warmed my nape. He followed me with the insistence of a much younger god, closing in on me, long before he felled me at the roots of those evergreens.

He kissed my face, my throat, my flushed earlobe. He pried apart my legs, rubbing against me and calling me by my only name. I threw back my arms. I turned my face up to God, the leaves, the moonless sky. Something in my manner must have struck him as tragic, for he took to repeating my name, softer, faster, as if sobbing or in prayer. His fingers scraped and prodded inside my underwear. He mauled and mouthed my tiny breasts through the thin stuff of my dress before realizing in his delayed, male way that all he had to do to get at them was to tug at a bit of string around my nape. Although he didn't know, with the death-bound certainty that I did, that this would be the last time, everything about his movements bespoke mourning, a heart as cankerous and worm-eaten as mine. When he emptied himself into me, there was no relief: only a more diffused kind of burning, which tingled from my toes to my lips to my fingertips, clutching at his spent, middle-aged flesh.

I would have given anything at that moment, to transform into cold wood within his arms, merging with the indifferent trees under which all this had occurred. He, however, had other ideas.

"'. . . e non se transformasse in verde selva . . .'," he whispered, stroking my hair, my arms, my breasts. "'. . . et non se transformasse . . .'"

"No more poetry, please," I said languidly. "I'm so sick of poetry."

"No more poetry," he agreed, even as he continued to commemorate and caress my immortal, too mortal body. He caressed me with the extreme tenderness that always proceeded from his exertions, no matter how rough these may have been. That evening, however, in the darkness of the woods, with no poetry to express the pain of our eternal parting, the tenderness of these caresses was redoubled. He caressed me until my body seemed to have no reality beyond his touch, until I felt myself to be entirely spirit. I lay silent beneath my god. I didn't want to be the first to shatter our divinity.

"Where, when?" he said at last. "Oh, my Daphne. When again?"

"In Arcadia. Always, in Arcadia."

EPILOGUE

Even in Arcadia, there are pills that bring about death. It was two days before my eighteenth birthday. I sat by the bedroom window, with its flickering white drapes, and lined the pills up beside a glass of tepid water. There were twelve of them in total—one for every month since I first met Steadman. I placed a pill on my tongue. I picked up the glass. In the distance, a car door slammed.

If I pictured heaven then, it was his car waiting in my driveway, with a full tank of gas and nowhere to go. It was skipping up to meet him with a bag on my shoulder. It was a burst of greenery, a rustling of leaves, my name on his lips.

My lips were dry. I looked down into the back garden. Beneath my window, the wisteria was swaying, its sweet scent wafting into my white room. In that moment, the distance from my bedroom to the drowning pool seemed too far, the greenness of the waters too sickening. I put down the glass. I remembered his words that first time, as he thrust himself into my greenness: *Do you want this? Do you want this?*

I remembered how sick I'd felt under his weight.

Since summer's beginning, my mother had been meaning to call in someone about the hornets' nest, which grew like a tumor among the wisteria. It was not until the Friday before my birthday that the exterminator arrived: a red-faced, pock-marked man a few years Steadman's junior. My mother and I stood beneath the pergola together, arms crossed as he assessed the situation. It was the closest that we had come to one another in weeks. "This is a big one," he clucked his tongue. "You really shouldn't have left it for so long. They're more aggressive in this heat." He wiped his hands on his bag-like white suit and told us that he could come back on Monday when it was due to be cooler, with a cocktail of rosemary oil, mint oil, and lauryl sulfate. My mother agreed. It struck me that I would have to move my suicide ahead by a day; that I couldn't possibly do what needed to be done with that man pottering around our garden.

It had been hot all through July and August. I spent my days by the drowning pool, in the shade of the willow, with an unread book or a wadded letter from Steadman. Against all my hopes, he never wrote to tell me that he couldn't go through with our plans; that he was still too in love with his wife; that his children needed him. Instead, I received long missives one or two times a week, rife with em dashes, sweet appellations, and the details of his latest job applications and sleeping arrangements. Reading about the nights that he passed in his home study, on a sagging single mattress, staring up at Byron and *Beata Beatrix*, my heart was stung, as if by a whole hive of hornets. My responses were infrequent, evasive. I copied out lines of poetry, stuffed envelopes with flowers and foliage. I wrote haiku.

A green girl shivers
Shadowy water spreads
A death before twilight.

At the end of July, he was offered a post at a coed day school. Though it was no Saint Cecilia's, he was sure that it would tide us over for the year. The divorce papers had been filed and the twins would no longer speak to him. With heartfelt apologies, he told me of California divorce laws, the six months that it would take for his marriage to be legally dissolved. He proposed a January wedding in Pennsylvania snow, among clusters of mountain laurel, my cold lips parted until death.

I did not tell him how much cause for hope those six months gave me; how I prayed that he hadn't ruined his life completely, for my sake. Likewise, he was not to know—at least from my pen—of the letter that I posted on Friday, after the hornet man's visit. This letter was addressed to Dr. Danielle Steadman of Larkspur, California, and has been transcribed below.

August 8, 2003

Carmel-by-the-Sea
Monterey County

Lady Steadman,

I pray that you will forgive me for taking the liberty of writing to you, although we have never been formally introduced. If what I have been told about you is true, then I may presume that you are a wise woman, a compassionate woman, a woman who will grant my words her gentle consideration. Even so, I am aware that what I am asking of you is the height of presumption; that you have no reason to show me any consideration, let alone mercy; that I am as low before you as any whore would be, before a lady of your virtues.

I have loved your husband—as much as a weak, heartless girl of my type is capable of loving. In return, he claims to love me, to the point that he wishes to start a life with me.

He wants a life with me. He does not realize that such a life is impossible; that I am, in fact, death.

Death can be pretty. It can be young fruit, blushing amid the branches. It can be lips and hair and bare legs. All the same, it is death, and should not be treated as anything other than such. It is not art, it is not poetry, and it is certainly not life.

Your husband has been foolish. He has allowed himself to be seduced by death, in the guise of a virgin. Please, do not hold this against him. You are his true wife, and he loves you, as he cannot possibly love anyone else. You have a life together. You have a son and a daughter and a greenhouse. Without this life, there is nothing left for him but death.

I do not doubt that he will come back to you. When he does, if you can, I beg that you forgive him. His sins are mortal, yet, unlike mine, they are forgivable; they need not extend to the grave.

Sincerely,

Ophelia (a drowning girl)

I HADN'T intended to still be alive when my letter reached Danielle Steadman, nor when the hornet man returned with his bag of poisons. That time around, we watched him from the safety of the poolside, equally transfixed by the removal of that malign growth. For two months, I had watched the nest grow at the same rate as my anxiety over Steadman's impending arrival. I stood beside my mother and hated her for being the cause of it all, the only one with the power to stop it. I began with the words that I had prepared a day earlier; words whose veracity I still cannot vouch for. "I didn't want it. I didn't want it at all . . ."

I T'S SPRING now in Pennsylvania and the Bryn Mawr girls can be seen walking around without stockings. I watch the prettiest ones go by over my coffee, which I drink black and with two sachets of sweetener. I'm still drinking it when I get to my mailbox, which I haven't checked since the beginning of the week. I spent last night in Dani's dorm and am running on only four hours of sleep. I remember tripping over her books in the dark this morning, Kristeva and Rilke and *The Tibetan Book of the Dead*. I remember her sighing and curling up deeper inside her nest of red sheets and strawberry blond hair. He'd probably appreciate the irony of me finding a Danielle of my own.

My tongue is still furred with the taste of her, acrid and persistent through the sweetness of my coffee. I don't know if I like this taste, but there's satisfaction in what it recalls. Dani's lips. Dani's hair. Dani, wet and glistening in the dark.

There are two envelopes waiting in my mailbox. The first is postmarked from California and is addressed in my mother's rounded, rather infantile hand. I haven't told her about Dani yet and am in no hurry to, though I'm sure she'll take the news easier than last spring's bombshell. The second envelope looks older. It boasts a foreign postmark and a charming, almost illegible scrawl of red ink. There is no return address.

I have trouble concentrating in my comparative-literature seminar, and not only from lack of sleep. In the pocket of my camel-hair coat, the unopened envelope burns, hot as a summons to hell. Of course, I haven't heard from him in months; not since he fled prosecution last fall. At the time, I thought his flight for the better. As soon as class is over, I rush out into the fresh April morning, my hands in my coat pockets. Here, I have no laurel groves to retreat to. I make do with crossing Merion Green and finding a place beneath the oaks. I breathe in and take out Steadman's letter.

April 10, 2004

Fiesole
Italia

Laurel—

Don't fret. This isn't a declaration of Lust. As far as you are concerned, I am a eunuch now—I haven't the heart or the balls to desire, anymore. The nymphs of Toscana are free to frolic around me. I'll look on coldly—if I look at all.

I had hoped for a new existence here. But my promised land is really more of a St. Helena. I don't know if my little life warrants such a grand Exile.

You will be finishing your first year of college, I suppose. I suppose you will have a boyfriend by now. It must be wonderful, having your whole life ahead of you. It must be wonderful, being free of my affections.

Europe seems to me such a dry, dead place. At least the nights are getting shorter now. I've taken to avoiding rooming houses altogether—there are better ways to spend what remains of my money. Sleeping out is not too unpleasant, in this climate. I've grown a beard, but don't feel too bad about this.

Were you never happy with me? Were my attentions misguided? Could I have been more tender? I don't suppose I'll ever get an answer, but I'm entitled to ask, at least. I remember us laughing about the illegality of it—as if <u>you</u> would never have anything to do with my ruin. Now I am

a "sex offender," a "perver," a "statutory rapist"—not
because of what I did, but because you were not ready to
take me seriously.

I think about Hell. I think about Heaven. I am done
wanting you. There is nothing more that I care to know about
you. Find a mild, faithful lover. It will be enough for you.

Yours,

Hugh

I fold up Steadman's letter and put it aside. I can feel
my insides squirming, my heart hammering inside my chest.
Closing my eyes, I lean my back against the oak's broad trunk,
and try to summon something of that old tenderness, but everything old is bitter. Everything old is repellent to me on this
fresh spring day.

Perhaps in Tuscany there are still nymphs that rise out
from the tree trunks, leading grown men astray. Perhaps there
are girls who defy death by dwelling outside life, in the greenness of old woods, young suicide. In Pennsylvania, however,
there are no nymphs—only college girls, who look just as good
as schoolgirls without their stockings. I am one of them. I rise
from the grass and brush the dirt from my raw knees, leaving
his letter behind for whatever wind or rain may come. I cross
the green.